FANTASTIC CREATURES

FIELD GUIDE TO
FANTASTIC CREATURES

GILES SPARROW

Quercus

CONTENTS

INTRODUCTION

This book takes you on the ultimate safari, around the world and through the imaginations of countless people from ancient times to the present day. Some of these fabulous and fantastical creatures have appeared in stories, dreams and nightmares around the globe. Some are mythical beings that probably never existed, some are fairytale creatures that live in a different reality to our own, and others, perhaps the most intriguing of all, may lie hidden from science, still awaiting official discovery even as they appear openly in folktales and the accounts of startled eyewitnesses. This Field Guide is your reference to all these strange creatures, and a vital aid as you set off on your global adventure.

These days no explorer should be without the latest equipment, and the guide uses sophisticated technology to immerse you in the world of fabulous creatures. Clever optical devices let you get close to the creatures without disturbing them (or endangering yourself!), and a range of digital displays provide you with plenty of extra information as you travel from location to location in search of these rare animals. In general, you'll be using three types of device – the binocular view, periscope view and data archive.

BINOCULAR VIEW

This versatile device allows you to view creatures up close without interfering with their normal behaviour. can be fitted to aircraft, submersibles or ground ehicles when needed for a quick getaway, and can lso be used as a remote camera operated from the afety of a distant 'hide'. The Field Guide uses a head-up' display to project a range of extra information about the creatures you're seeing without interfering with your view.

DISTRIBUTION MAP

A changing regional map indicates the location of monster sightings, or the regions where myths and legends associated with an animal originated.

DYNAMIC TIMELINE

This historic record displays significant events in the story of the creature – eyewitness sightings, close encounters and important written accounts.

DATA POP-UPS

Additional information appears in pop-up boxes overlaid on your main viewport.

WESTERN DRAGON

Of all the world's fantastic creatures, the dragon is probably the most famous, and certainly the most majestic. It is found in two distinct subspecies – the ferocious, dinosaur-like western dragon and the more benign, serpent-like eastern or Chinese dragon. Western dragons are famed for a number of attributes, such as high intelligence (some have even been said to speak) and the ability to breathe fire. They also had a tendency, at least in medieval times, to hoard treasure and kidnap local maidens.

This compact viewing device is especially useful for observing creatures that are aggressive, but it also allows you to watch more timid animals without disturbing them. Working like a submarine periscope, it lets you get a close-up view while you stay safely hidden in a vehicle or camouflaged hide. The periscope viewer can be fitted with a range of devices such as night vision equipment and a zoom lens. To keep the picture clear, the Field Guide displays most of the additional data outside of your main field of view.

RISK ASSESSMENT

This display indicates the potential risk level – even apparently harmless creatures can have a dangerous side.

ENVIRONMENT AND DIET

Data readouts give information on the creature's preferred living conditions and eating habits.

TRACKING TIPS

This data display provides useful information that can help to track and identify the creature.

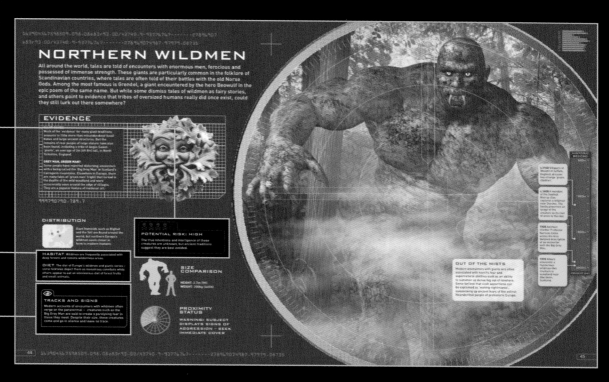

NORTHERN WILDMEN

All around the world, tales are told of encounters with enormous men, ferocious and possessed of immense strength. These giants are particularly common in the folklore of Scandinavian countries, where tales are often told of their battles with the old Norse Gods. Among the most famous is Grendel, a giant encountered by the hero Beowulf in the epic poem of the same name. But while some dismiss tales of wildmen as fairy stories, and others point to evidence that tribes of oversized humans really did once exist, could they still lurk out there somewhere?

EVIDENCE

Much of the evidence for many great traditions amounts to little more than misunderstood local tales and large ancient structures. But the remains of real people of large stature have also been found, including a tribe of Anglo-Saxon 'giants', an average of 2m (6ft 9in) tall, in North Yorkshire, England.

GREY MAN, GREEN MAN
Some people have reported disturbing encounters with a being called the 'Big Grey Man' in Scotland's Cairngorm mountains. Elsewhere in Europe, there are many tales of 'green men' (right) that lurked in the depths of the wild woodland and were occasionally seen around the edge of villages. They are a popular feature of medieval art.

DISTRIBUTION

Giant hominids such as Bigfoot and the Yeti are found around the world, but northern Europe's wildmen seem closer to links to modern humans.

HABITAT Wildmen are frequently associated with deep forests and remote wilderness areas.

DIET The diet of Europe's wildmen and giants varies – some historians depict them as monstrous cannibals while others appear to eat an omnivorous diet of forest fruits and small animals.

TRACKS AND SIGNS

Modern accounts of encounters with wildmen often verge on the paranormal – creatures such as the Big Grey Man are said to create a paralysing fear in those they meet. Despite their size, these creatures come and go in silence and leave no trace.

POTENTIAL RISK: HIGH
The true intentions and intelligence of these creatures are unknown, but ancient traditions suggest they are best avoided.

SIZE COMPARISON
HEIGHT: 2.7m (9ft)
WEIGHT: 200kg (440lb)

PROXIMITY STATUS
WARNING: SUBJECT DISPLAYS SIGNS OF AGGRESSION – SEEK IMMEDIATE COVER

OUT OF THE MISTS
Modern encounters with giants are often associated with mist or fear and supernatural abilities such as an ability to summon up dense fog out of nowhere. Some believe that such apparitions can be explained in waking nightmares or swimming up ancient fears of the extinct Neanderthal people of prehistoric Europe.

DATA ARCHIVE

Some creatures are just too elusive to track down even with the cleverest modern technology, while others are sadly lost in the past. Fortunately, the Field Guide is equipped with a comprehensive digital archive that allows you to access records on even these creatures, including artists' impressions, eyewitness encounters, and other useful information.

TROLLS AND OGRES

European folklore is full of tales of monstrous giants, trolls and ogres. Trolls come from the Scandinavian countries and are split into two breeds – large, hairy and barbaric monsters of the far north and smaller, more human-like creatures (often with tails) further to the south. The larger breed of troll is similar to the fearsome, sometimes man-eating, ogre of French, German and English fairy stories.

Trolls first appear in Viking epic poems or sagas from the 9th century. Rather like fairies and the djinns of Arabia (see p.14), they seem to be mostly invisible to humans, going about their own lives and only occasionally coming into contact with people. They are often seen as thieves, stealing crops, livestock and other supplies from remote farmhouses, and hoarding treasure. But in most tales they are not truly wicked, simply living by a different set of rules and, like fairies, punishing humans who break those rules. Their other fairy-like habits include abducting people and sometimes stealing newborn babies to leave their own offspring (so-called 'changelings') in their place.

Trolls may have started out as 'hidden people' (Huldufólk) similar to fairies, but fairytales of the Middle Ages turned them into more ferocious and thoroughly wicked monsters, with a taste for human flesh. These later trolls are often indistinguishable from ogres found in Britain, France and Germany.

Although the word ogre was invented by poets in the 12th century, the first real ogres were monsters called Gog and Magog that lived in Cornwall, in the west of England, long before the first people arrived in the British Isles.

Ogres are usually portrayed as harrendous man-eating giants, slow-witted but sometimes with magical powers. The most famous of these traditional ogres is surely the one encountered by Puss in Boots, the feline hero of an old French fairy tale written down by Charles Perrault in the late 1600s. This monster lives in a castle, terrorizing the land for miles around, and has the power to transform himself into other animals. The cunning Puss tricks him into changing into a mouse and then eats the ogre while he is powerless.

In recent times, as fear of trolls and ogres has receded, stories such as Shrek have taught us to be more sympathetic to these strange giants. Although frequently bad-tempered and often difficult to understand, they may not be as terrible as the storytellers of the Middle Ages would have us believe.

DISTRIBUTION
Trolls live in Iceland and Scandinavian countries, such as Sweden and Norway. Ogres are usually found in southern central and western Europe.

An illustration by Swedish artist John Bauer shows a large troll surprised as it goes about its business.

EVIDENCE

TROLLS IN THE LANDSCAPE
Travel in Norway or Iceland today and the locals will happily point out the signs of trolls in the countryside. Some hills and rock formations are described as petrified trolls, perhaps turned to rock by exposure to daylight, while other strange hills are thought to be the homes of trolls. Like other magical creatures, trolls are often found near water crossings and of course are famous for lurking beneath bridges in fairytales. In Iceland especially, trolls and their cousins the elves are widely respected and considered so real, if invisible, neighbours. Building projects, for example, are sometimes altered to avoid harming the elves.

This illustration by Reginald Knowles shows a member of the smaller and more ornate Scandinavian troll subspecies.

SIZE COMPARISON
HEIGHT: 3.5m (11ft 8in)
WEIGHT: 260kg (600lb)

IMAGE ARCHIVE

These pop-ups display interesting historical images and supplementary information about them.

SCALE INDICATOR

This box provides an instant guide to the general size of the target creature, along with other vital statistics such as length, wingspan and weight.

LEGENDS AND EVIDENCE

This screen offers additional information about the target animal – physical evidence and intriguing theories, or the complex legends that lay behind some creatures.

STRANGE WORLD

Stories of fantastic creatures are found all around the world and throughout history. Wherever you travel, it's easy to find tales of local monsters or animals that are not recognized by science, but getting to the truth behind these stories can be much harder.

Some, it seems, are myths that developed from ancient religions, or the inventions of storytellers whose names have long since been forgotten even while their creations live on. Others may have begun life as misunderstood descriptions of normal animals or the cultures of other peoples, distorted as they have been handed down from one generation to the next.

But many defy explanation – and some of these may be tales of real undiscovered animals. While finding the truth behind most stories is a job for experts in myth and legend, discovering the reality behind these creatures is a task for explorers and zoologists. The scientific quest for these beasts has its own name – cryptozoology ('the science of hidden animals').

Cryptozoologists are real-life monster hunters, travelling to remote parts of the world in the hope of unearthing the truth behind local legends, and perhaps finding new species of animal as a result.

In this day and age, it might seem impossible for large animals to remain undiscovered by science, but the truth is rather different. Thousands of new species are still being found each year, and while most are tiny insects, there are occasional spectacular exceptions. As recently as 1992, zoologists in Vietnam discovered a large forest ox called the saola – who knows what else is still hidden? It's time to find out.

THE AMERICAS

Monsters of North and South America range from beasts of Native American and Mesoamerican legend, to supernatural apparitions and apparently physical animals that are still unknown to science.

MONSTERS OF SEA AND AIR

Some of the largest fantastic creatures roam the world's oceans and air currents, free from the bounds of geography. They range from huge sea monsters to insubstantial atmospheric beasts.

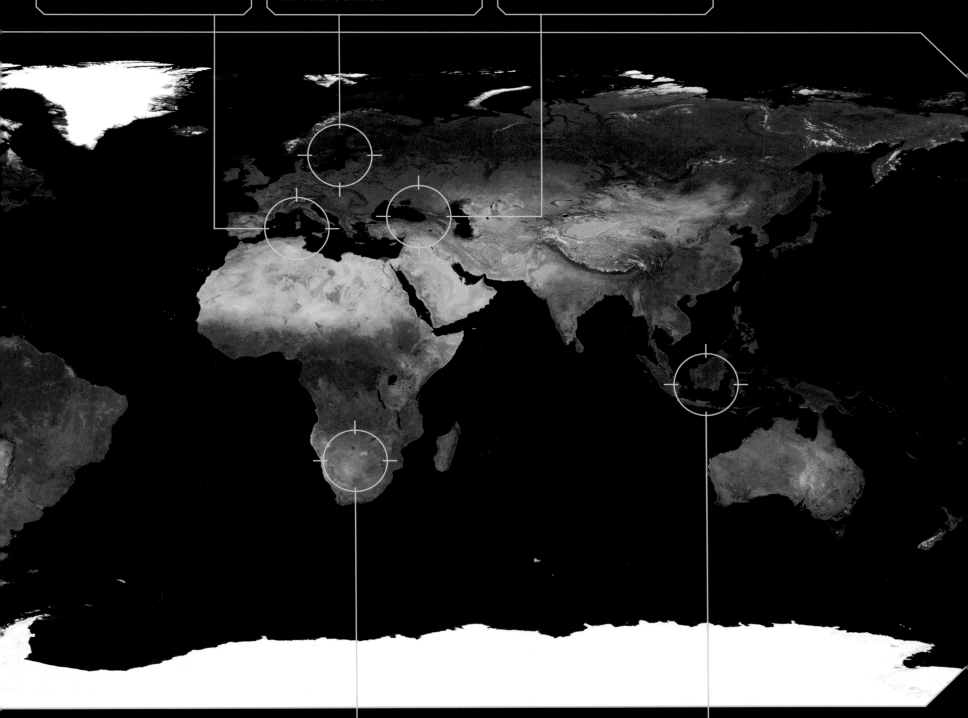

MEDITERRANEAN MONSTERS

The fertile lands bordering the Mediterranean Sea were home to great ancient civilizations whose legendary creatures still survive in our imaginations to this day.

NORTHERN EUROPE

Away from the Mediterranean, the nations of Europe have their own rich heritage of fabulous beasts, ranging from fairytale monsters to supernatural beings and elusive animals.

OUT OF THE EAST

The lands of the Middle East are home to some of the most ancient creatures of our imagination – monsters that have lived alongside us since the dawn of civilization itself.

AFRICAN BEASTS

Africa's fantastic creatures are less well documented than those in other parts of the world. But they are just as intriguing, since they seem to include some fascinating relics from the prehistoric past.

ASIA AND BEYOND

The continents of Asia and Australasia and the islands in between them are home to a huge variety of creatures that range from living legends to prehistoric survivors.

D4567598509.098.08e83r93.00/43740.9-93776767------27896907
93.00/43740.9-93776767------278969074987.97979.08735

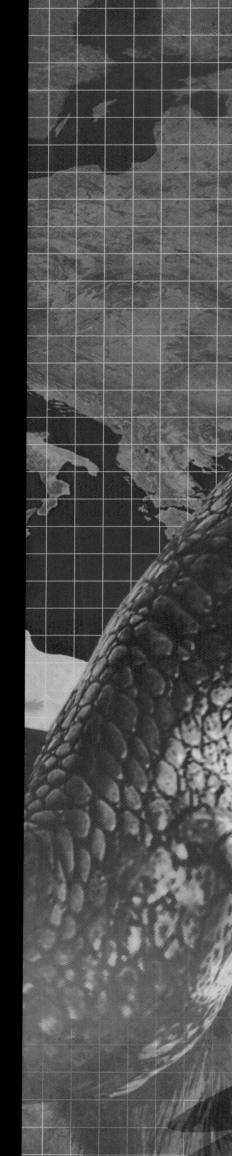

OUT OF THE EAST

People have written stories of monsters and other fabulous beasts since the dawn of recorded history – and probably told similar tales around the fireside long before writing was invented. The most ancient of these creatures that we know about come from Mesopotamia – the land between the Tigris and Euphrates rivers in present-day Iraq, where the first civilizations were established more than 5000 years ago. These beasts of the Middle East may have changed their form over time, as they made their appearances in books as diverse as the Bible and the *Arabian Nights*, but they are still with us today in the shape of dragons, giant birds, sea monsters and genies.

DISTRIBUTION

The *sirrush* is known from the mythology of Babylon and Mesopotamia, but the animal itself may have originated in Africa.

THE SIRRUSH

Two and a half thousand years ago, King Nebuchadnezzar of Babylon in modern-day Iraq built a mighty monument as the centrepiece of his city. He decorated the towering Ishtar Gate with images of sacred bulls, lions – and a curious dragon-like creature with the forelimbs of a lion, the hindlegs of an eagle and the body of a serpent. This animal is known as the *sirrush* or *mushhushshu* (both names translate as 'splendour serpent'). It has puzzled archaeologists and cryptozoologists alike since the ruins of Babylon were first excavated in the early 20th century. The artists placed it alongside real, rather than mythical, animals. So could it have been a real dragon – and might it still exist?

300
250
200

AUTO 150

100

50

0

EVIDENCE

KOLDEWEY AT BABYLON

German archaeologist Robert Koldewey, who dug up the ruins of Babylon in the early 1900s, was the first person to suggest that the *sirrush* might be a living creature. One of his arguments was that depictions of the *sirrush*, unlike those of other mythical animals, rarely changed.

BEL AND THE DRAGON

According to a Biblical text called *Bel and the Dragon*, Nebuchadnezzar planned to sacrifice the Hebrew prophet Daniel to a dragon kept in a temple at Babylon, but Daniel killed the beast by feeding it poisoned barley cakes. Could this have been a living *sirrush*?

TRACKS AND SIGNS

The *sirrush* is noted for its lion-like front legs, and the ornate crest and horn on its head. If Babylonian images are accurate, and its forelimbs and hindlimbs are so radically different, then it should certainly leave distinctive tracks!

PROXIMITY STATUS

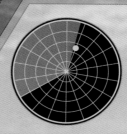

SUBJECT CALM BUT CURIOUS – OBSERVE BUT DO NOT PROVOKE

HABITAT The only descriptions of the *sirrush* place it in captivity, but if it was indeed a sauropod dinosaur, then it probably survived in a jungle habitat.

DIET If stories of Daniel poisoning Nebuchadnezzar's dragon with barley cakes are true, then the *sirrush* was probably vegetarian rather than carnivorous.

A LIVING DINOSAUR?

Cryptozoologist Willy Ley suggested that images of the *sirrush* were quite close to those of sauropod dinosaurs. Is it possible that the Babylonians had captured a creature such as *Mokele-Mbembe* (see p.118) from Africa and brought it to their city?

...OR A FOSSIL ONE?

Another theory is that Nebuchadnezzar's dragon was an early attempt at reconstructing a fossil dinosaur. If bits of several different animals were muddled up in the process, it might explain the *sirrush*'s strange mix of features.

HISTORIC RECORD

1000 BC
500 BC
0 AD
500 AD
1000 AD
1500 AD
2000 AD

PRESENT DAY

c.575BC Nebuchadnezzar constructs the Ishtar Gate in Babylon.

c.125BC The story of *Bel and the Dragon* is written down, based on earlier traditions.

1902 Robert Koldewey rediscovers the Ishtar Gate.

SIZE COMPARISON

HEIGHT: 3m (10ft)
LENGTH: 5m (15ft)
WEIGHT: 1200kg (2400lb)

POTENTIAL RISK: LOW

Although Nebuchadnezzar made sacrifices to his beast, the evidence points to the *sirrush* being a harmless vegetarian, and an unfortunate victim of Daniel's poisoning scheme. Despite this, the animal's talons and defensive horn mean it should not be taken for granted.

16390456759850¶.098.08e83r93.00/43740.9-93776767------278969074987.97979

BEHEMOTH AND LEVIATHAN

The Bible is scattered with references to three great legendary beasts of enormous size and power. These are Behemoth, a gigantic grazing land beast, Leviathan, a fearsome serpentine sea monster, and the lesser-known Ziz, a huge bird whose wings are broad enough to block out the Sun.

The main source of information about these strange monsters is the Old Testament Book of Job, which spends two chapters describing Behemoth and Leviathan. Behemoth is an enormous grazing animal with powerful muscles and a massive tail, described as 'plundering the river' and 'lying in the reeds and the swamp'. Leviathan, meanwhile, is a 'twisted serpent' with scales that shield it from harpoons.

Finally, the Ziz is a creature of *midrash* – Jewish folklore that does not appear in the 'official' Bible. Aside from its enormous wingspan it is said to lay eggs the size of mountains and to be a protector of other birds. According to other stories, God created these giant creatures in pairs during the early days of the Earth, but then, realizing that if allowed to breed freely they would destroy the world, he killed one of each, so that now only one of each monster survives.

People have puzzled over the true identities of these Biblical giants for centuries. Some say they are entirely mythical beasts, representatives of the elements of earth, water and air. They may even have been 'borrowed' from other religions, since the early civilizations of Mesopotamia (modern-day Iraq) have a similar group of monsters known as the Hadhayosh, Kar and Simurgh.

Another idea is that these are exaggerated or misunderstood reports of real creatures. Bible scholars have often suggested that the hippopotamus is a good match for the description of Behemoth, and that Leviathan might be a whale or giant squid. The Ziz, meanwhile, has been compared to the ostrich and the extinct elephant bird of Madagascar (both of which lay enormous eggs). But there are problems with all of these matches – they don't explain Behemoth's tail, Leviathan's scales, or the fact that the Ziz is clearly able to fly, while the ostrich and elephant bird are flightless and spend their whole lives on the ground.

But there's one other possibility – perhaps the Bible was describing real animals that are still unknown to science? Some say that Behemoth sounds a lot like a giant sauropod dinosaur – perhaps even the *Mokele-Mbembe* of the African jungles (see p.118). Leviathan, of course, is a typical sea serpent (see p.100), and the Ziz could be linked to the Roc or even the North American thunderbird (see pp.18 and 90).

DISTRIBUTION

The location of these enormous beasts is unknown – just one of many mysteries surrounding them.

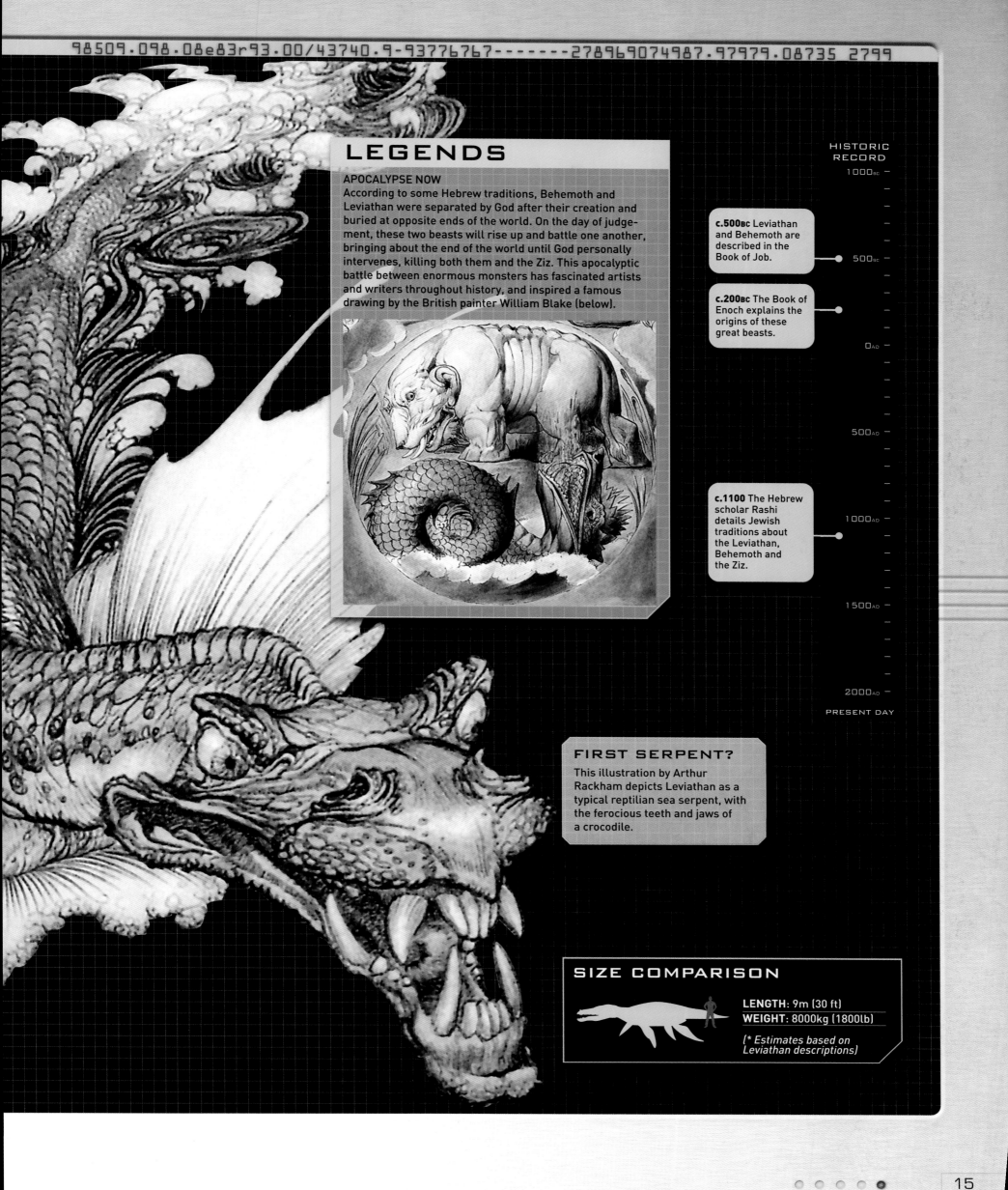

LEGENDS

APOCALYPSE NOW

According to some Hebrew traditions, Behemoth and Leviathan were separated by God after their creation and buried at opposite ends of the world. On the day of judgement, these two beasts will rise up and battle one another, bringing about the end of the world until God personally intervenes, killing both them and the Ziz. This apocalyptic battle between enormous monsters has fascinated artists and writers throughout history, and inspired a famous drawing by the British painter William Blake (below).

HISTORIC RECORD

1000BC

c.500BC Leviathan and Behemoth are described in the Book of Job.

500BC

c.200BC The Book of Enoch explains the origins of these great beasts.

0AD

500AD

c.1100 The Hebrew scholar Rashi details Jewish traditions about the Leviathan, Behemoth and the Ziz.

1000AD

1500AD

2000AD

PRESENT DAY

FIRST SERPENT?

This illustration by Arthur Rackham depicts Leviathan as a typical reptilian sea serpent, with the ferocious teeth and jaws of a crocodile.

SIZE COMPARISON

LENGTH: 9m (30 ft)
WEIGHT: 8000kg (1800lb)

(* Estimates based on Leviathan descriptions)

DISTRIBUTION

Djinns are found throughout modern Islamic cultures and particularly among the desert lands of the Middle East.

DJINNS

Since pre-Islamic times, the peoples of the Middle East have believed in a shadow realm of invisible beings who inhabit deserts and wastelands. According to Islamic tradition, these djinns or genies are nature spirits created from pure fire, and can be good or evil. They have their own society and usually follow their own desires and quarrels, being only dimly aware of people. However, the boundary between the human and djinn worlds can be bridged by black magic. Evil djinns can possess people, conjure storms and take a range of forms for mischievous purposes.

300

250

200

AUTO 150

100

50

0

LEGENDS

PERSIAN ORIGINS
Djinns seem to have originated in ancient Persia as evil female spirits called *jaini* that were thought to spread disease. With the arrival of Islam, djinns of both sexes were recognized and they were no longer seen as entirely evil.

ALADDIN AND HIS LAMP
The most famous djinn is undoubtedly the genie of the lamp in the story of Aladdin, as told in the *Arabian Nights*. This powerful spirit conjured up riches and a beautiful palace for the young thief who rubbed the lamp to which it was magically bound. But when the lamp fell into the hands of an evil sorcerer, Aladdin had to call on the aid of a lesser genie to save the day.

TRACKS AND SIGNS

Djinns are mostly shadowy beings that can remain invisible to humans, but they can take on forms ranging from dust storms to animals and humans (although they cannot perfectly copy the human form).

POTENTIAL RISK: MEDIUM

Although djinns cannot physically harm humans, they have the ability to possess them and can also cause a person to harm themselves through deception. However, djinns have personalities as varied as those of people – some can be actively helpful, but most have no interest in human affairs.

PROXIMITY STATUS

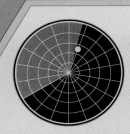

WARNING: SUBJECT MATERIALIZING – MAINTAIN CAUTION

HABITAT Most djinns prefer lonely places – deserts and wastelands away from human settlement – although some prefer to live closer to humans.

DIET Although they have little physical substance, djinns still need food to sustain themselves. They may steal from humans, take scraps from leftovers, or even take bones from cemeteries.

HISTORIC RECORD

0 AD

c.300 Ruins near Palmyra in Syria preserve inscriptions giving thanks to *ginnaye* for their kindness.

500 AD

c.633 The Prophet Mohammed includes a chapter about the djinn in Islam's holy book, the Qu'ran.

c.810 The first edition of the *One Thousand and One Nights* (*Arabian Nights*) compiles various tales of the djinn.

1000 AD

1500 AD

1704–17 Frenchman Antoine Galland translates the *Arabian Nights*, introducing genies to Europe for the first time.

2000 AD

PRESENT DAY

DUST DEMON

Since ancient Egyptian times, dust devils and towering sandstorms have been associated with djinns and related spirits. Desert travellers taking shelter from these sudden and dangerous events often report hearing the howls of the djinns that drive them.

SIZE COMPARISON

HEIGHT: 6m (20ft)
WEIGHT: Insubstantial

THE ROC

This gargantuan bird of prey is famous from the legendary tales of Sinbad the Sailor and the more factual accounts of Italian traveller Marco Polo. It is truly enormous, supposedly capable of carrying off elephants and killing them by dropping them to their doom on the ground below. But could such a monstrous winged beast ever have existed, and if not, what are the origins of the story? Perhaps it is linked to the remains of giant eagles and other enormous birds found in Africa, New Zealand and elsewhere.

300

250

200

AUTO   150

100

50

0

EVIDENCE

TRAVELLER'S TALE
Genoese merchant Marco Polo introduced the Roc to European audiences through his widely read *Travels*. According to Polo, the Chinese believed this giant bird inhabited the island of Madagascar. Later stories, such as the *Arabian Nights'* tale of sailors who find a Roc's egg (above), secured the Roc's place in the imagination of western readers.

TRUE GIANTS
More recently, the Roc has been dismissed as a fantasy, but this certainty has been shaken by the discovery that an enormous eagle, with a wingspan of 3m (10ft), did indeed survive on Madagascar until the 1500s. It fed on other extinct giant animals such as the flightless elephant bird and giant lemurs. A bird of similar size hunted New Zealand's moas until around the same time.

FREQUENT FLIER

Despite its immense size, the Roc spends almost its entire life on the wing. Yet according to Chinese traditions, this skilled aerial predator starts life as a fish-like water monster, only taking to the air when it reaches adulthood.

PROXIMITY STATUS

SUBJECT AIRBORNE AT HIGH SPEED – IMMEDIATE EVASIVE ACTION REQUIRED!

HABITAT According to Arabic traditions, the Roc soars across Asia and the Indian Ocean on high air currents, only ever landing at its nest, traditionally said to be on the mountain of Qaf at the centre of the world.

DIET The Roc supposedly lives on the remains of elephants and other large animals, which it abducts and then kills by dashing to the ground.

☠ ☠ ☠ ☠ ☠

POTENTIAL RISK: MEDIUM

According to the *Arabian Nights'* tales of Sinbad and the Roc, humans are so small that this giant bird ignores them. However, Rocs are said to destroy ships by dropping boulders on them, perhaps mistaking them for more substantial food such as whales.

TRACKS AND SIGNS

The Roc comes and goes in near-silence, only attracting attention when its enormous shadow passes overhead. Roc eggs are highly prized and immense, as befits such as an enormous bird.

HISTORIC RECORD

1000AD

1100AD

1200AD

1298 Marco Polo describes Mongol traditions about the Roc in an account of his travels in China.

1300AD

1300s Earliest surviving copies of the *One Thousand and One Nights* (*Arabian Nights*) include tales of Sinbad the Sailor and the Roc.

1400AD

1500AD

1400–1500 Giant eagles on New Zealand and Madagascar become extinct.

PRESENT DAY

SIZE COMPARISON

HEIGHT: 6m (20ft)
WINGSPAN: 30m (100ft)
WEIGHT: 1000kg (2200lb)

01001101
10011101
010000

6360387·080·0·3278646584940q------999790790·789·7---8789468968940·0·0

16390456759850q.09&.08e83r93.00/43740.9-93776767------27&96907
e83r93.00/43740.9-93776767------278969074987.97979.08735

MEDITERRANEAN MONSTERS

The ancient civilizations of Egypt, Greece and Rome all surrounded the Mediterranean Sea, influencing each other over the course of 2,000 years or more. Each had its own rich tradition of monsters, gods and supernatural beasts – ferocious monsters such as the Chimera and Sphinx, mystical creatures such as the phoenix and the flying horse Pegasus, and strange, almost-human beings such as the centaurs and satyrs. The stories of human heroes and their encounters with these various beasts have been told and retold over the centuries and still fuel our imaginations today – the monsters of the Mediterranean can still be found, if you know where to look for them.

16390456759850q.09&.08e83r93.00/43740.9-93776767------

16390456759850 9.098.08e83r93.00/43740.9-93776767------27896907
e83r93.00/43740.9-93776767------2789690749 87.97979.08735

THE CHIMERA

A ferocious mixture of lion, goat and snake, the Chimera has given its name to the English language as a word for any kind of hybrid animal. The real fire-breathing monster is said to lurk among the volcanic vents of Mount Chimaera in Lycia, a region of southwest Turkey. According to Greek myth, it shared its ancestry with other many-headed monsters including the Hydra and Cerberus. Sightings of this beast are said to be an omen of shipwrecks and natural disasters including storms and volcanic eruptions.

LEGENDS

BELLEROPHON'S TALE

In Greek mythology, the Chimera was slain by the hero Bellerophon. An exiled prince, Bellerophon was wrongly accused of attempting to ravish the daughter of King Iobates. Unwilling to break the rules of hospitality by killing a guest in cold blood, Iobates sent the unwary Bellerophon to slay the Chimera – a task he thought would mean certain death.

MISSION IMPOSSIBLE

With the help of the Goddess Athena, Bellerophon tamed the winged horse Pegasus, and rode him to battle with the fire-breathing monster. Unable to pierce the Chimera's impenetrable hide, Bellerophon had an ingenious idea – he mounted a piece of lead on the end of his spear and rammed it down the creature's throat. The flames melted the lead and the Chimera choked to death.

999790790.789.7

DISTRIBUTION

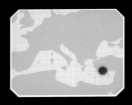

The Chimera is a unique beast, found only on the slopes of Mount Chimaera in southwestern Turkey.

HABITAT: The animal is seldom seen, but is believed to lurk amid permanently burning vents of volcanic gas known in Turkish as the *Yanartas* (flaming rock).

DIET: The Chimera's diet is unknown, though it may nourish itself on methane from the volcanic vents themselves.

TRACKS AND SIGNS

With roughly a dozen burning flames emerging from the harsh volcanic terrain, the *Yanartas* are easily seen from the Turkish coast, and are a popular destination for hikers. However, sightings of the Chimera have been rare in recent times.

POTENTIAL RISK: EXTREME

With an impervious hide, ferocious fangs, and the ability to breathe fire, the Chimera is a vicious hunter. Three heads also make it hard to approach unseen.

SIZE COMPARISON

HEIGHT: 1.8m (6ft)
LENGTH: 3m (10ft) head to head
WEIGHT: 90kg (200lb)

PROXIMITY STATUS

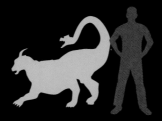

WARNING: SUBJECT HIGHLY AGGRESSIVE – RETREAT IMMEDIATELY!

MONSTROUS ANCESTRY

The Chimera was one of the many monstrous offspring of Echidna and Typhon. These two creatures, partly human and partly dragon, spawned countless other beasts in the early days of the world.

HISTORIC RECORD

1500BC

c.800BC Homer describes the Chimera.

1000BC

c.700BC Hesiod writes about the origins of the Chimera in his *Theogeny*.

500BC

c.100BC An unknown author summarizes the story of Bellerophon and the Chimera in the *Biblioteca*.

0AD

PRESENT DAY

MONSTERS OF MYTH

Greek mythology is filled with fantastical monsters in a huge variety of forms. Some of these creatures are purely imaginary, while others seem to have a hint of reality about them. They include fabulous and exaggerated forms of known animals, as well as completely new creatures, and some peculiar tales that seem impossible to explain but are backed up by surprising amounts of archaeological evidence.

Some of the best-known monsters in Greek legend are the ones encountered by the great hero Hercules as he struggled to achieve his twelve mythical labours. The first of these tasks was to kill the ferocious Nemean Lion, famed for its impervious skin. The second was to slay the hydra, a nine-headed water serpent that regrew two heads for each one that the mighty warrior lopped off.

Other fabulous beasts encountered by Hercules during his tasks included the dangerous Erymanthian Boar, the man-eating Stymphalian Birds, the fleet-footed Golden Hind of Artemis, and the many-limbed giant Geryon. The final task was to capture Cerberus, the enormous, slavering three-headed dog that guarded the gates of Hades, the Greek underworld. Cerberus in particular is a popular adversary in various Greek myths – returned to his rightful place by Hercules at the end of his labours, the hound was later encountered by Orpheus, who lulled it to sleep with his lyre (an ancient musical instrument) in order to enter Hades in search of the spirit of his lost wife Eurydice.

There are many other monsters elsewhere in Greek myth – famous ones include the Minotaur (see p.34) and Medusa (see p.38). The disinherited prince Jason and his famous crew of 'argonauts'

steered their ship, the Argo, between two huge living rocks (the Cyanean rocks) that threatened to crush them, and had to cope with many other monstrous encounters during their quest for the famed Golden Fleece. This fleece was the wool of a sacred ram, perhaps laden with gold after being used for sifting tiny flecks of gold out of streams. Revered in the kingdom of Colchis (modern-day Georgia) on the Black Sea, this fabulous treasure was watched over by a dragon that never slept. It could only be overcome with a potion provided by the sorceress Medea, daughter of the local king Aeetes.

SIZE COMPARISON

LENGTH: 5m (18 ft)
WEIGHT: 1000kg (2200lb)

The three heads of Cerberus could supposedly see the past, present and future. This made Hercules' challenge of capturing the monstrous dog even more difficult.

98509.098.08e83r93.00/43740.9-9377676?------278969074987.97979.08735 2799

LEGENDS

SERPENTS IN THE GARDEN

In order to reach the Golden Fleece, Jason needed the assistance of Orpheus, who played music to soothe the Colchian dragon, and Medea, who then used her magic to send it to sleep (right). This monster kept watch in a grove sacred to Ares, the god of war, and other dragons in Greek myth also seem to have a liking for gardens. Hercules had to outwit a serpent called Ladon in order to collect golden apples from the Garden of the Hesperides at the western edge of the world and another dragon, Ismenios, watched over the sacred spring near Thebes. Ismenios and the Colchian dragon seem to be related, since they share magical powers – in both cases their teeth were later sown across barren ground and produced fearsome warriors called *spartoi*.

DISTRIBUTION

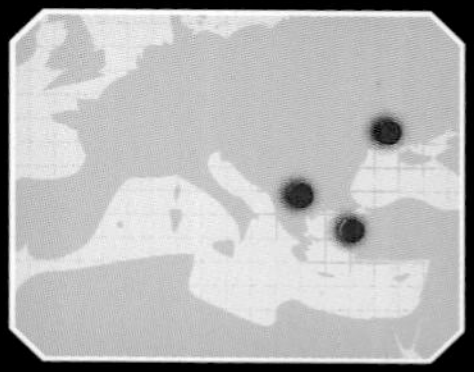

These various monsters live around the fringes of the Mediterranean Sea – the edges of the known world in ancient Greek times.

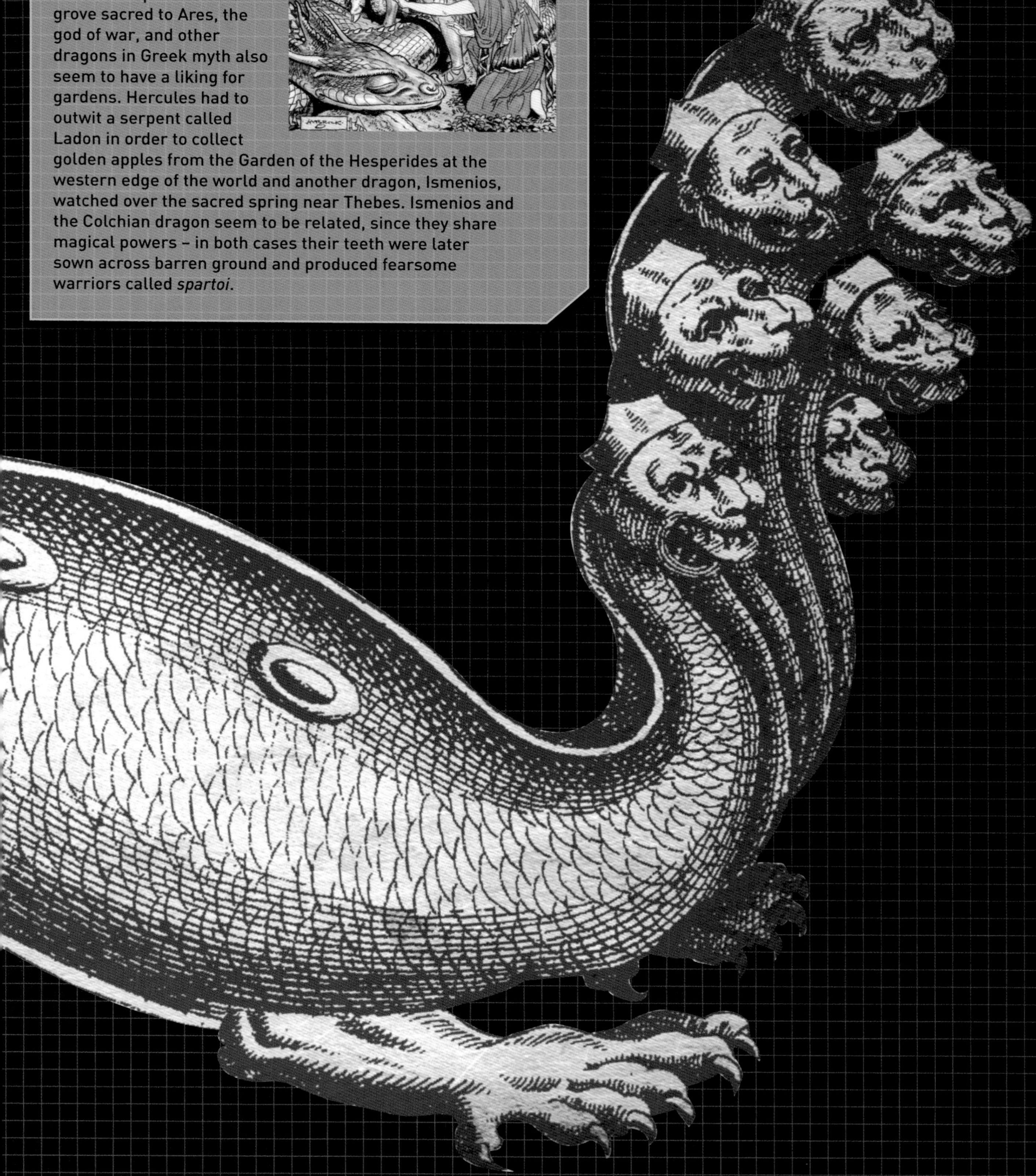

HISTORIC RECORD

1000BC

c.800BC The great poet Homer writes encounters between the hero Ulysses and a variety of monsters in his *Odyssey*.

c.700BC Greek writer Hesiod lists the origins of many ancient monsters in his *Theogeny*.

c.600BC Greek poet Peisander writes the definitive list of Hercules' labours in a lost poem.

500BC

c.250BC Apollonius of Rhodes writes down the legend of Jason and the Argonauts, based on earlier accounts.

0AD

PRESENT DAY

25

THE MANTICORE

A Persian equivalent of the Egyptian sphinx, the manticore is a fabulous mixture of animals. It is usually described as having a human face armed with rows of vicious teeth, the body of a lion, the wings of a bat and a scorpion's sting on its tail. Its name derives from the old Persian for 'man eater' – it has a trumpeting voice, and like the sphinx, is said to challenge its victims with a riddle before consuming them. Manticores were said by the ancient Greeks to live in the jungles of India, where they preyed on many different animals. Some think that this description is actually a misinterpretation of the tiger.

LEGENDS

EARLY ACCOUNTS
The first description of the manticore comes from the Greek writer Ctesias, writing in the 4th century BC. Based on what he learned from Persian contacts, he described the 'Martikhora' as a tiger-sized beast capable of discharging stings from its scorpion-like tail.

MEDIEVAL POPULARITY
After Roman historian Pliny the Elder included the beast in his influential book on natural history, the manticore became a popular creature in the medieval animal books known as bestiaries. There it was seen as a symbol of envy, deceit and tyranny.

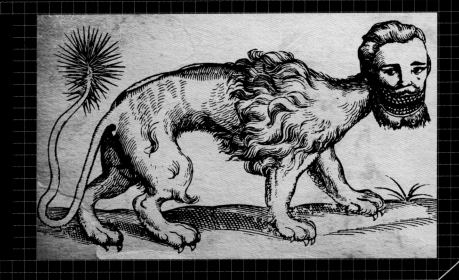

999790790.789.7

DISTRIBUTION

While the Persians insisted the manticore was an Indian beast, its origins may lie among earlier mythical Mesopotamian beasts.

HABITAT The manticore is said to live in jungles, sometimes hiding in an underground lair.

DIET With its three rows of ferocious teeth, the manticore is almost always depicted as a man-eating monster.

TRACKS AND SIGNS

The manticore's call is said to be midway between that of a pipe organ and a trumpet. It is capable of mimicking human speech, even if tales of its riddling ability are exaggerated.

POTENTIAL RISK: EXTREME

With a powerful lion-like body, stinging tail, fearsome set of teeth and deceiving nature, the manticore is not a creature to be trusted.

SIZE COMPARISON

HEIGHT: 1.5m (5ft)
LENGTH: 4m (13ft)
WEIGHT: 200kg (440lb)

PROXIMITY STATUS

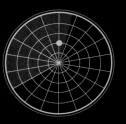

WARNING: SUBJECT WITHIN FIRING RANGE – USE SAFETY SHIELDING

STING IN THE TAIL

According to Persian descriptions, the manticore's sting is capable of shooting out barbs some 30cm (1ft) long. They can kill any animal smaller than an elephant. When confronted directly, the beast holds its tail back over its head to fire these lethal darts towards its attacker.

HISTORIC RECORD

c.400BC Ctesias of Cnidus, physician to Persian king Artaxerxes II, first describes the manticore.

c.79AD Roman naturalist Pliny the Elder writes about the manticore in his *Natural History*.

c.200 Roman author Claudius Aelianus provides a more detailed description of the manticore.

500BC

0AD

500AD

PRESENT DAY

HISTORIC RECORD

c.730BC Hesiod describes the birth of Pegasus in his *Theogeny*.

1000BC

c.430BC Greek playwright Euripides describes the story of Pegasus and Bellerophon in a play that has since been lost.

500BC

0AD

c.150AD Greek geographer Pausanias recounts myths of springs formed where Pegasus's hooves struck the ground.

500AD

∨
∨
∨
∨
∨

PRESENT DAY

MAGIC HOOVES

According to several legends, fresh springs erupted wherever the flying horse touched the ground. On Mount Helicon in Boeotia, for instance, there are two springs named the Hippocrene and the Aganippe, both formed in the hoof-prints of Pegasus.

16390456759850S.098.08e83r93.00/43740.9-93776767------27896907

e83r93.00/43740.9-93776767------278969074987.97979.08735

PEGASUS

The winged horse of Greek legend is among the most famous of all fabulous creatures. But horses capable of flight are found in legends around the world and there are still occasional reports of sightings to this day. Pegasus supposedly sprang from the remains of Medusa after she was slain by Perseus (see p.38). He features in several other myths of the Greek heroes, most famously that of Bellerophon, who rode him in his battles against the female Amazon warriors and the multi-headed Chimera.

LEGENDS

PEGASUS AND BELLEROPHON

Bellerophon captured Pegasus using a golden bridle given to him by the goddess Athena (right), but after his victory over the Chimera, he aimed to fly the winged horse to Mount Olympus, the home of the gods themselves. Zeus, king of the Greek gods, sent a gadfly to sting Pegasus, causing the horse to rear and Bellerophon to plunge back to Earth. Zeus kept the winged horse for himself and eventually preserved him as a constellation in the sky.

CLOSE RELATIVES?

According to the Qu'ran, the winged horse al-Buraq carried the Prophet Mohammed from Mecca to Jerusalem. Other cultures also have their own winged horse legends. For the Turkic people of central Asia, it is called *Tulpar*, while *Chollima* is a Korean equivalent.

999790790.789.7

TRACKS AND SIGNS

On the ground, the traces of winged horses cannot be easily distinguished from those of their ordinary brethren, while in flight they leave no signs at all. However, it is said that a Pegasus feather once fell to Earth near the city of Tarsus in modern Turkey.

DISTRIBUTION

Winged horse legends are found across Europe and Asia. Some speculate that the horse-headed 'Jersey Devil' of the United States (see p.84) is a similar creature.

HABITAT Flying horses can live in a variety of wild areas – they may be solitary or join herds of normal horses.

DIET As far as we know, winged horses have the same food requirements as normal horses, grazing freely on grass and other vegetation.

SIZE COMPARISON

HEIGHT: 2.1m (7ft)
WINGSPAN: 6m (20ft)
WEIGHT: 500kg (1100lb)

POTENTIAL RISK: LOW

Flying horses shy away from humans, but anyone attempting to approach one should be wary of their quick tempers and tendency to lash out.

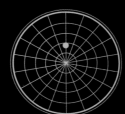

PROXIMITY STATUS

SUBJECT IN FLIGHT – MAINTAIN SAFE DISTANCE AND OBSERVE

16390456759850 9.098.08e83r93.00/43740.9-93776767------27896907
e83r93.00/43740.9-93776767------278969074987.97979.08735

THE CYCLOPS

Greek and Roman mythology contains many tales of fearsome one-eyed giants known as cyclopes, usually described as living on remote islands or in other distant parts of the world. They range from Polyphemus, the lone cyclops that menaced the Greek hero Ulysses and his crew on their long journey home from the Trojan War, to the Arimaspians, a race of one-eyed warriors who waged a long battle with the gryphons of central Asia (see p.122). Are these ferocious wildmen the product of overactive Greek imaginations, or do they have an origin in reality?

EVIDENCE

ULYSSES AND POLYPHEMUS

In Homer's epic poem *The Odyssey*, Ulysses and his crew put ashore on the island of the cyclopes and take shelter in a cave that turns out to be the lair of the giant Polyphemus. Returning home with his sheep, he blocks the cave entrance trapping the crew. In order to escape, they get the cyclops drunk and blind him with a stake, before escaping by tying themselves to the underside of his sheep as they are let out to graze.

ONE-EYED ELEPHANTS?

Many experts believe that the legends of the cyclops were inspired by the skulls of dwarf elephants (right) that once lived on Mediterranean islands. The large nasal cavity where the trunk joins the skull could easily be mistaken for an enormous eye socket.

999790790.789.7

DISTRIBUTION

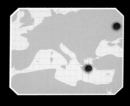

The island of the cyclopes lies in an unspecified part of the Mediterranean, while the Arimaspians were said to be a central Asian tribe.

HABITAT These fearsome giants typically favour pastures and beaches with nearby caves to store their sheep.

DIET The cyclops is a voracious meat eater, farming sheep. But it is also happy to eat humans or even its own kind.

TRACKS AND SIGNS

These one-eyed giants can be detected from their enormous footprints and the abandoned remains of their meals – they are notoriously messy eaters.

POTENTIAL RISK: HIGH

Cyclopes are savage wildmen with enormous stature and brute strength on their side. However, lack of intelligence means they can sometimes be outwitted.

SIZE COMPARISON

HEIGHT: 7m (24ft)
WEIGHT: 11,000kg (24,000lb)

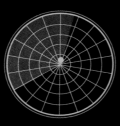

PROXIMITY STATUS

SUBJECT EXTREMELY AGGRESSIVE – MAINTAIN HEIGHT AND OBSERVE

PEGASUS

The winged horse of Greek legend is among the most famous of all fabulous creatures. But horses capable of flight are found in legends around the world and there are still occasional reports of sightings to this day. Pegasus supposedly sprang from the remains of Medusa after she was slain by Perseus (see p.38). He features in several other myths of the Greek heroes, most famously that of Bellerophon, who rode him in his battles against the female Amazon warriors and the multi-headed Chimera.

LEGENDS

PEGASUS AND BELLEROPHON
Bellerophon captured Pegasus using a golden bridle given to him by the goddess Athena (right), but after his victory over the Chimera, he aimed to fly the winged horse to Mount Olympus, the home of the gods themselves. Zeus, king of the Greek gods, sent a gadfly to sting Pegasus, causing the horse to rear and Bellerophon to plunge back to Earth. Zeus kept the winged horse for himself and eventually preserved him as a constellation in the sky.

CLOSE RELATIVES?
According to the Qu'ran, the winged horse *al-Buraq* carried the Prophet Mohammed from Mecca to Jerusalem. Other cultures also have their own winged horse legends. For the Turkic people of central Asia, it is called *Tulpar*, while *Chollima* is a Korean equivalent.

999790790.789.7

TRACKS AND SIGNS

On the ground, the traces of winged horses cannot be easily distinguished from those of their ordinary brethren, while in flight they leave no signs at all. However, it is said that a Pegasus feather once fell to Earth near the city of Tarsus in modern Turkey.

DISTRIBUTION

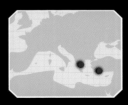

Winged horse legends are found across Europe and Asia. Some speculate that the horse-headed 'Jersey Devil' of the United States (see p.84) is a similar creature.

HABITAT Flying horses can live in a variety of wild areas – they may be solitary or join herds of normal horses.

DIET As far as we know, winged horses have the same food requirements as normal horses, grazing freely on grass and other vegetation.

SIZE COMPARISON

HEIGHT: 2.1m (7ft)
WINGSPAN: 6m (20ft)
WEIGHT: 500kg (1100lb)

POTENTIAL RISK: LOW

Flying horses shy away from humans, but anyone attempting to approach one should be wary of their quick tempers and tendency to lash out.

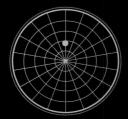

PROXIMITY STATUS

SUBJECT IN FLIGHT – MAINTAIN SAFE DISTANCE AND OBSERVE

163904567598509.098.08e83r93.00/43740.9-93776767------278969074987.97979

HALF-HUMANS

Many fantastic creatures from the ancient world have features that are partly human, partly animal. They had a particular fascination for ancient peoples, perhaps because they lived much closer to nature than we do today. The Greeks were particularly keen on stories of these hybrid creatures, often telling tales that warned against giving in to the animal part of human nature.

These half-human beasts are as varied in their temper, attitude and motivation as any normal person – they range from monstrous harpies and sirens to mischievous satyrs and fauns.

But the best known of all these strange creatures are probably the centaurs – a race of noble but fiery tempered people with the hindquarters and legs of horses, and the upper body of a human. They were famous for their drunken ways and their battles with an ancient Greek tribe called the Lapiths. However, their leader Chiron was famous for his intelligence and great wisdom. As a result, he became tutor to many of the great Greek heroes, including Theseus, Hercules and Jason.

The fawns and satyrs are quite similar creatures, with the upper body of a human and goat-like legs. They can usually be told apart because satyrs have human feet and are usually large and muscular, while fauns are small and lithe, with hooved feet. The satyrs were followers of Dionysus, the Greek god of merrymaking. The fauns were their Roman equivalents, creatures that also loved to drink and followed the wine god Bacchus, but eventually transformed into rather more timid nature spirits, though they seem to have kept their mischievous sense of humour.

While centaurs and satyrs can at least be reasoned with, some other half-human creatures are much more aggressive, ruled entirely by their animal nature. The harpies, for instance, were huge and ravenous birds with the heads of women. In order to punish King Phineas of Thrace for misusing his talent for prophecy, Zeus, the king of the Greek gods, imprisoned him on an island where he was constantly pestered by harpies. Every day an enormous banquet was laid out before the King, but the bird-women constantly snatched the food from his hand before he ever got the chance to eat it.

Perhaps related to harpies, the sirens were another race of birds with female heads. They were famed for an alluring song, which lured many a sailor to stray too close to their remote island. Once wrecked on their rocky shores, these poor wretches soon fell victim to the man-eating sirens, who feasted on their flesh. Jason and the Argonauts only survived their encounter with the sirens because the musician Orpheus drowned out their song with the beautiful music from his lyre.

EVIDENCE

BIZARRE ENCOUNTERS
It's comforting to imagine the half-human creatures of ancient myth as safely lost in the past, but some people claim to have had shocking encounters with these strange animals far more recently. Cryptozoologists tend to dismiss reports of fauns and satyrs as mistaken sightings of more likely wildmen, but sightings of human-headed horses, such as the one seen in County Louth, Ireland in 1966 are harder to explain. The Scots also tell tales of a harpy-like creature called the Skree, which was seen before the bloody battle of Culloden in 1746 and is said to appear before battles foretelling death and destruction.

SIZE COMPARISON

LENGTH:
2.5m (8ft)

WEIGHT:
400kg (900lb)

98509.098.08e83r93.00/43740.9-9377b767------278969074987.97979.08735 2799

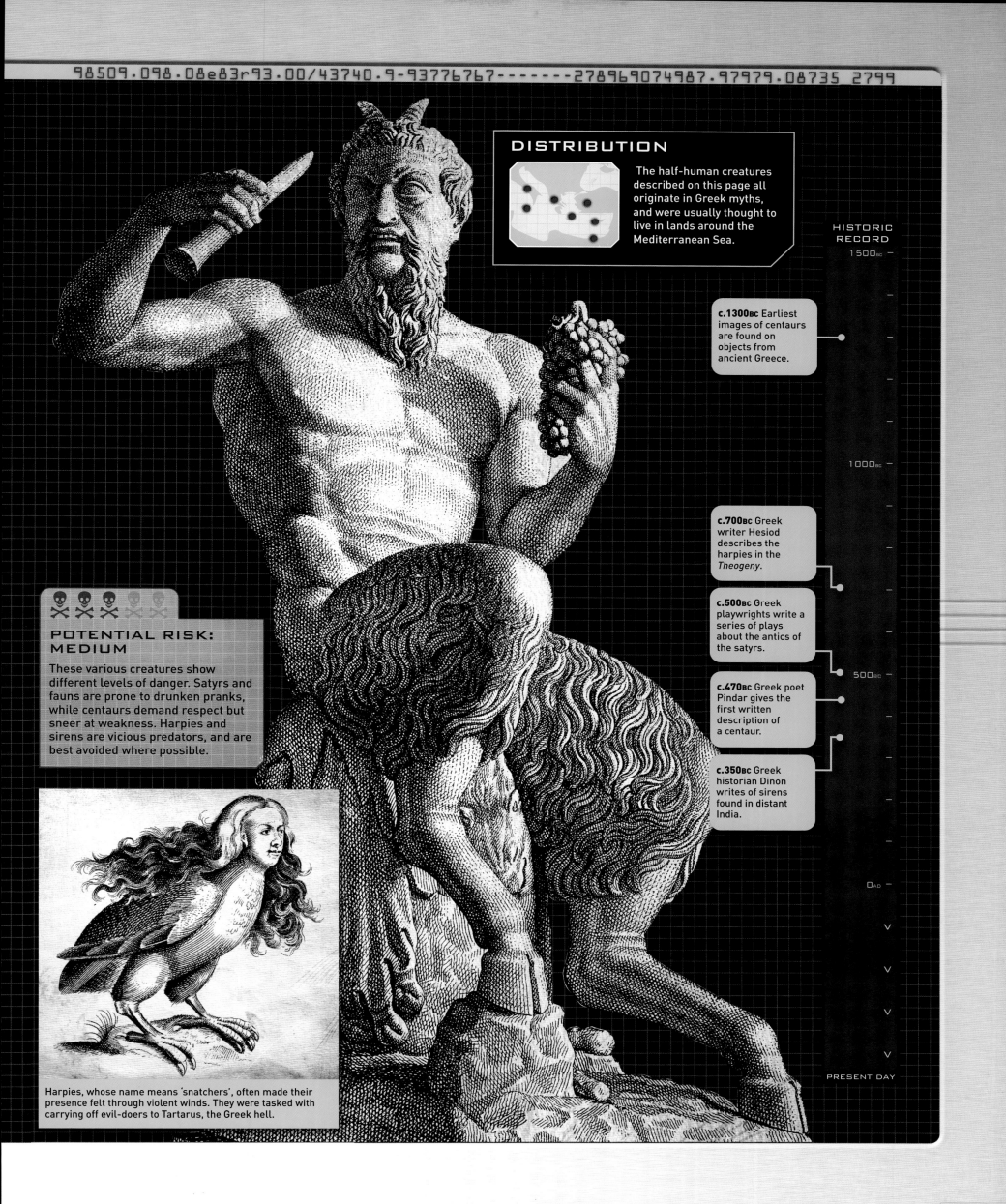

DISTRIBUTION

The half-human creatures described on this page all originate in Greek myths, and were usually thought to live in lands around the Mediterranean Sea.

POTENTIAL RISK: MEDIUM

These various creatures show different levels of danger. Satyrs and fauns are prone to drunken pranks, while centaurs demand respect but sneer at weakness. Harpies and sirens are vicious predators, and are best avoided where possible.

Harpies, whose name means 'snatchers', often made their presence felt through violent winds. They were tasked with carrying off evil-doers to Tartarus, the Greek hell.

HISTORIC RECORD

1500ʙᴄ

c.1300ʙᴄ Earliest images of centaurs are found on objects from ancient Greece.

1000ʙᴄ

c.700ʙᴄ Greek writer Hesiod describes the harpies in the *Theogeny*.

c.500ʙᴄ Greek playwrights write a series of plays about the antics of the satyrs.

500ʙᴄ

c.470ʙᴄ Greek poet Pindar gives the first written description of a centaur.

c.350ʙᴄ Greek historian Dinon writes of sirens found in distant India.

0ᴀᴅ

PRESENT DAY

THE CYCLOPS

Greek and Roman mythology contains many tales of fearsome one-eyed giants known as cyclopes, usually described as living on remote islands or in other distant parts of the world. They range from Polyphemus, the lone cyclops that menaced the Greek hero Ulysses and his crew on their long journey home from the Trojan War, to the Arimaspians, a race of one-eyed warriors who waged a long battle with the gryphons of central Asia (see p.122). Are these ferocious wildmen the product of overactive Greek imaginations, or do they have an origin in reality?

EVIDENCE

ULYSSES AND POLYPHEMUS
In Homer's epic poem *The Odyssey*, Ulysses and his crew put ashore on the island of the cyclopes and take shelter in a cave that turns out to be the lair of the giant Polyphemus. Returning home with his sheep, he blocks the cave entrance trapping the crew. In order to escape, they get the cyclops drunk and blind him with a stake, before escaping by tying themselves to the underside of his sheep as they are let out to graze.

ONE-EYED ELEPHANTS?
Many experts believe that the legends of the cyclops were inspired by the skulls of dwarf elephants (right) that once lived on Mediterranean islands. The large nasal cavity where the trunk joins the skull could easily be mistaken for an enormous eye socket.

999790790.789.7

DISTRIBUTION

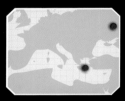

The island of the cyclopes lies in an unspecified part of the Mediterranean, while the Arimaspians were said to be a central Asian tribe.

HABITAT These fearsome giants typically favour pastures and beaches with nearby caves to store their sheep.

DIET The cyclops is a voracious meat eater, farming sheep. But it is also happy to eat humans or even its own kind.

TRACKS AND SIGNS
These one-eyed giants can be detected from their enormous footprints and the abandoned remains of their meals – they are notoriously messy eaters.

POTENTIAL RISK: HIGH
Cyclopes are savage wildmen with enormous stature and brute strength on their side. However, lack of intelligence means they can sometimes be outwitted.

SIZE COMPARISON

HEIGHT: 7m (24ft)
WEIGHT: 11,000kg (24,000lb)

PROXIMITY STATUS

SUBJECT EXTREMELY AGGRESSIVE – MAINTAIN HEIGHT AND OBSERVE

MASTER BUILDERS

According to Greek legends, the three original cyclops were brothers whose massive size allowed them to build huge monuments. They were also blacksmiths, forging thunderbolts for Zeus.

HISTORIC RECORD

1000BC

c.800BC Homer tells the tale of Ulysses and the cyclops Polyphemus in *The Odyssey*.

c.700BC Greek historian Hesiod describes the origin of the cyclops race in his *Theogeny*.

500BC

c.275BC Sicilian poet Theocritus writes of Polyphemus' unfulfilled desire for the sea nymph Galatea.

0AD

PRESENT DAY

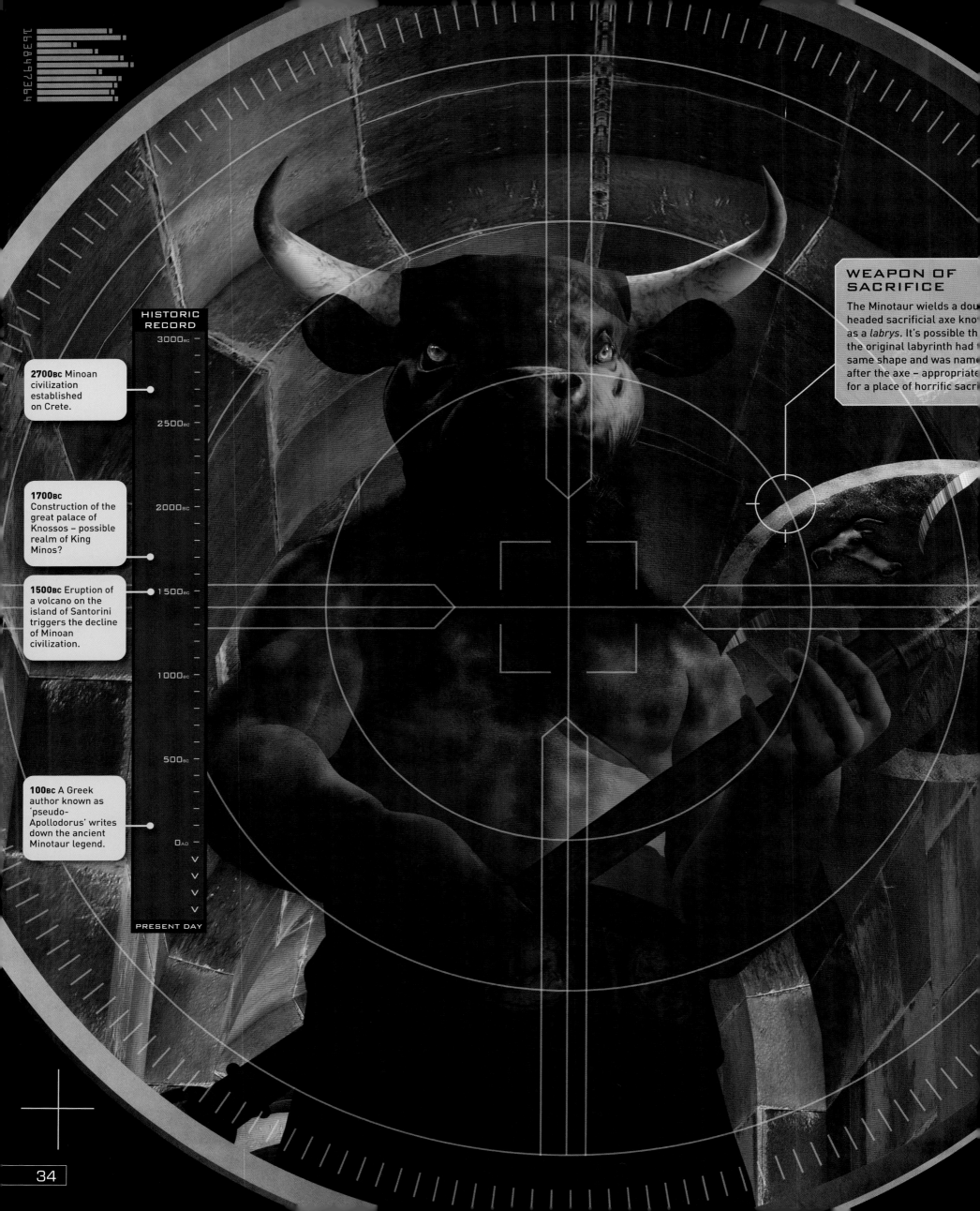

HISTORIC RECORD

3000BC

2700BC Minoan civilization established on Crete.

2500BC

1700BC Construction of the great palace of Knossos – possible realm of King Minos?

2000BC

1500BC Eruption of a volcano on the island of Santorini triggers the decline of Minoan civilization.

1500BC

1000BC

500BC

100BC A Greek author known as 'pseudo-Apollodorus' writes down the ancient Minotaur legend.

0AD

∨
∨
∨
∨
∨

PRESENT DAY

WEAPON OF SACRIFICE

The Minotaur wields a dou... headed sacrificial axe kno... as a *labrys*. It's possible th... the original labyrinth had ... same shape and was nam... after the axe – appropriate... for a place of horrific sacri...

THE MINOTAUR

Ancient Greek myths tell of a monstrous creature with the body of a man and the head of a bull, kept by King Minos of Crete in an impenetrable labyrinth beneath his palace at Knossos. Minos fed this Minotaur with a periodic sacrifice of seven youths and maidens demanded from Athens, but Theseus, son of the Athenian king, travelled with the sacrifices. Aided by the Cretan princess Ariadne, he killed the Minotaur and found his way back out of the labyrinth. The original Minotaur is supposedly long dead, but there are other bull-headed gods in ancient myth – who knows what really lies behind the story?

LEGENDS

ORIGINS OF THE MINOTAUR
The Minotaur was the hideous son of Queen Pasiphae, cursed by the gods to fall in love with a bull in order to punish a broken vow by her husband Minos. The king and queen attempted to raise the hybrid child, but as it grew stronger and wilder they built the labyrinth to contain it.

DIGGING UP THE LABYRINTH
When British archaeologist Arthur Evans dug up the remains of Knossos (right) in the 1930s, he found remarkable signs that the ancient civilization of Minoan Crete had indeed treated bulls as sacred animals (right) and may have practised human sacrifice.

999790790.789.7

TRACKS AND SIGNS
The Minotaur is a subterranean beast at home in the semi-darkness of the labyrinth, but can be traced by its stench and the sound of its heavy breathing.

DISTRIBUTION

While the original Minotaur came from the island of Crete in the Mediterranean, bull-headed gods are common across Europe and Asia.

HABITAT The Minotaur was confined in a labyrinth that, once entered, could not be escaped. Theseus made his way back out by marking his route in with a ball of twine given to him by the princess Ariadne.

DIET According to the legend, the Minotaur developed a taste for human flesh.

SIZE COMPARISON

HEIGHT: 8ft (2.5m)
WEIGHT: 160kg (350lb)

POTENTIAL RISK: EXTREME
Possessed of immense strength and the short temper of a wild animal, the Minotaur is a vicious killer and close encounters should be avoided.

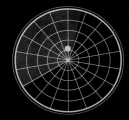

PROXIMITY STATUS

WARNING: SUBJECT DISPLAYS RISING AGGRESSION – RETREAT SLOWLY

16390456759850九.098.08e83r93.00/43740.9-93776767------278969074987.97979

THE SPHINX

With the body of a lion and the head of a woman, the Sphinx is perhaps the most instantly recognizable of all fantastic creatures. It is preserved in art across the ancient world, including the largest statue of all, at Giza in Egypt. Yet the Sphinx is a hybrid animal in more ways than one – later Greek storytellers grafted their own legend onto a much earlier Egyptian creation.

Egyptian sphinxes first appeared during the so-called 'Old Kingdom' period, when the first truly powerful pharaohs ruled the kingdom around the River Nile. The Great Sphinx at Giza was probably built by the Pharaoh Djedefra around 2500BC, perhaps as a monument to his father Khufu, who had built the Great Pyramid some years before. This human-headed, lion-bodied statue proved so iconic that it helped to establish the Sphinx as an emblem of Egypt, copied countless times in temples and monuments. Often these later sphinxes were modified with portraits of current pharaohs or the heads of other animals. These could be associated with particular regions or specific gods (most Egyptian deities were represented by human figures with animal heads). The lion body, however, remained a constant and came to be associated with the lion Sekhmet, a powerful goddess of the Sun.

Strangely, we don't know what the Egyptians themselves called these distinctive statues. But as their imagery spread around the Mediterranean, they soon reached Greece, where they were named after a mythological monster that already existed – the Sphinx.

This demonic creature, whose name means 'strangler', has the head and torso of a woman and the body of a lion. It sometimes also has the wings of an eagle and tail of a serpent. According to legend, she sat on a high rock guarding the approach to the Greek city of Thebes, demanding that all travellers who passed by attempt to answer her riddle: 'What animal goes on four legs in the morning, two legs at noon and three legs in the evening?' When travellers failed to guess the answer, the sphinx pounced, strangling and devouring them. She was finally defeated by the Greek prince Oedipus, who proclaimed that the answer was 'a man, who crawls as an infant, walks upright in the prime of life and uses a stick in old age'. Frustrated, the Sphinx flung herself from the rock to her death – the victorious Oedipus later became king of a grateful Thebes.

Sphinxes are also found elsewhere around the world, especially across south Asia, where they are popular figures in Hindu and Buddhist art. Known by a variety of names, they are often seen as protective deities, warding off evil spirits and bringing good fortune.

98509.098.08e83r93.00/43740.9-93776767------278969074987.97979.08735 2799

EVIDENCE

MYSTERIES OF THE SPHINX

The first European tourists to visit Egypt in the 1600s found that only the great head of the Sphinx was visible above the sand. The statue's enormous body was only fully revealed in 1925. Since the 19th century, however, the Sphinx has attracted a huge variety of theories about its origin and purpose. Some say that it is far older than the pyramids, and that the Egyptians modified an earlier lion statue with the head of their pharaoh. Others claim that the beast's body hides secret chambers, perhaps with a library of lost knowledge. Though there is no way of proving any of these claims, the Sphinx today still attracts thousands of visitors.

3000bc —

c.2500bc The 4th-Dynasty pharaoh Djedefra builds the Great Sphinx at Giza.

2500bc

2000bc —

c.1400bc Pharaoh Thutmose IV clears away the sand that has already buried most of the Giza Sphinx.

1500bc

c.700bc Greek historian Hesiod describes the origin of the Greek Sphinx in his *Theogeny*.

1000bc

500bc

c.467bc Greek playwright Aeschylus writes a trilogy of plays telling the story of Oedipus and featuring the Sphinx.

0ad —

A Greek illustration of Oedipus' encounter with the Sphinx reveals that the original creature was far smaller than its statues.

PRESENT DAY

DISTRIBUTION

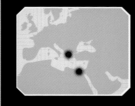

Traditions of a Sphinx-like creature seem to have arisen independently in Egypt and Greece.

SIZE COMPARISON

LENGTH: 2.1m (7ft)
WEIGHT: 180kg (400lb)

163904567598509.098.08e83r93.00/43740.9-93776767------27896907
e83r93.00/43740.9-93776767------278969074987.97979.08735

MEDUSA

With writhing hair of living snakes, the gorgons were three ferocious sisters, supposedly cursed by the Greek goddess Athena. Most terrifying of all was Medusa, a once-beautiful maiden transformed into a creature with the tail of a monstrous serpent and a gaze so fearsome that just one glance was enough to turn people to stone. Traditional Greek myths claim that Medusa was soon slain by the hero Perseus, but can we be sure – and what became of her sisters? Could they still lie waiting in their subterranean home beneath Mount Olympus?

LEGENDS

PERSEUS AND MEDUSA
The best-known story about Medusa comes from her appearance in the ancient Greek legend of Perseus. The young hero was sent to retrieve the gorgon's head by King Polydectes, who wanted Perseus out of the way so he could forcibly marry the boy's mother. Perseus slew Medusa, using a mirror given to him by Athena in order to avoid meeting her deadly gaze and chopping off her head. On his way back home, he encountered the Princess Andromeda, tied to a rock by her parents in an attempt to appease an enormous sea monster. Perseus used Medusa's head to turn the monster to stone. He returned to Polydectes' court with the princess, where he was enraged to find his mother turned into the king's serving drudge. He then unveiled Medusa's head before the disbelieving king and his court, turning them to stone in an instant.

999790790.789.7

DISTRIBUTION

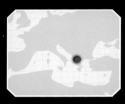

The gorgons are said to live beneath Mount Olympus in northern Greece.

HABITAT These hideous sisters dwell in deep caves beneath the mountain, never emerging into the daylight.

DIET The gorgons' diet is unclear – perhaps they hunt small mammals, relying on surprise to ensure their prey never gets a chance to look them in the eye.

TRACKS AND SIGNS

Their deadly gaze makes gorgons extremely difficult to hunt, but the story of Perseus and the mirror suggests that night-vision goggles or other optical devices will not transmit their petrifying power.

POTENTIAL RISK: EXTREME

With their terrible gaze and vicious claws and fangs, gorgons are highly dangerous and should be approached with extreme caution.

SIZE COMPARISON

HEIGHT: 1.8m (6ft)
LENGTH: 5m (16ft)
LENGTH: 180kg (400lb)

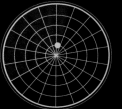

PROXIMITY STATUS

WARNING: SUBJECT ALERT AND HOSTILE – RETREAT AND AVOID DIRECT EYE CONTACT

SNAKEHEAD

In some Greek tales, Medusa's ferocious gaze and serpentine hair were the work of Athena, goddess of wisdom, who was angered to find her beautiful handmaiden in the arms of the sea god Poseidon. Surprisingly, images of the gorgon's head were used as protective emblems across the classical world.

HISTORIC RECORD

1000bc

c.800bc Greek poet Homer makes a passing reference to the terrible power of a gorgon's gaze in his epic *Iliad*.

500bc

c.700bc Greek historian Hesiod introduces the idea of three gorgon sisters in his *Theogeny*.

0ad

c.150bc Apollodorus of Athens writes a summary of the myth of Perseus and Medusa.

PRESENT DAY

16390456759850g.098.08e83r93.00/43740.9-93776767------278g6g074g87.97g7g

THE PHOENIX

A fabulous firebird whose story is told in tales from across the ancient world, the phoenix lives for 500 years. When approaching death, it regenerates itself through burning and rising from its own ashes. The earliest stories of a phoenix-like bird come from Egypt and India, but there are independent tales of a similar bird from Greece, China and Japan.

The idea of an immortal bird is curiously widespread throughout ancient civilizations. One theory is that all the different forms of phoenix trace their origin back to an ancient eagle-like bird god associated with the Sun. Just as the Sun appears to go through its own life cycle in each year as the length of days changes, perhaps this 'solar bird' was also thought to die and be 'reborn' each midwinter.

The earliest tales of a phoenix-like bird come from ancient Egypt, where the purple heron or benu was associated with the Sun god Ra. Some said that these birds sprang from the flames of a sacred burning tree, while others claimed that the original benu had arisen from the great god Osiris when he rose from the dead. These birds were treated with special reverence at Heliopolis, the City of the Sun, and their temple was used to measure the position of the Sun and keep the Egyptian calendar.

The word phoenix comes from the ancient Greek and means 'shining one' – the poet Hesiod was the first to use the name and mention the bird's famously long life. But the full story of its life cycle was only outlined by the historian Herodotus. He described the bird's red and gold plumage in detail (although he admitted he had never seen it himself), and explained how it normally lived in India and only came to Egypt once in every 500 years. At that time the old phoenix died and a new, identical one hatched from a burning egg of fire.

Russian folklore has its own phoenix-like bird, known as the *zhar-ptitsa* or Firebird. This beautiful bird with plumage that glows in the colour of flames is said to herald the spring, make the flowers bloom and bring good luck. But those who try to catch it often find themselves cursed by bad luck until they restore its freedom. Some say that all of these birds are descendants of the *Simurgh*, a fabulous bird in ancient Persian legends, said to be so long-lived that it had seen the destruction and rebirth of the world three times over.

DISTRIBUTION

The original phoenix came to Egypt from India, but related birds are found in Russia, China and Japan.

98509.098.08e83r93.00/43740.9-93776767------27896074987.97979.08735 2799

SIZE COMPARISON

WINGSPAN:
1.5m (5ft)
WEIGHT:
1.8kg (lb)

LEGENDS

THE CHINESE PHOENIX

The sacred bird of China is often called the Chinese phoenix, but its true name is the *fenghuang*, and it has little in common with the true phoenix of the Mediterranean region. According to tradition, it is the queen of the birds, a hybrid with the head of a pheasant, the body of a duck, the wings of a swallow and the tail of a pheasant. Although it does not go through the same cycle of life and death as the phoenix, the *fenghuang* is also associated with fire and the Sun. It is seen as a symbol of virtue and good luck, and was often used to represent the Chinese Empress, alongside the dragon as a symbol of the Emperor.

HISTORIC RECORD

c.800BC The Egyptian *Book of the Dead* refers to a phoenix-like bird called the *benu*.

c.700BC Hesiod is the first to mention the phoenix by name, and to describe its long lifespan.

c.440BC Greek writer Herodotus describes the life cycle of the phoenix in his *Histories*.

c.170AD Flavius Philostratus writes his own account of the life cycle of the phoenix.

1000BC

500BC

0AD

500AD

PRESENT DAY

The ageing phoenix is said to build its nest and funeral pyre from twigs of myrrh, a resinous wood that was widely believed to have magical properties.

63904567598509.098.08e83r93.00/43740.9-93776767------27896907
83r93.00/43740.9-93776767------278969074987.97979.08735

NORTHERN WILDMEN

All around the world, tales are told of encounters with enormous men, ferocious and possessed of immense strength. These giants are particularly common in the folklore of Scandinavian countries, where tales are often told of their battles with the old Norse Gods. Among the most famous is Grendel, a giant encountered by the hero Beowulf in the epic poem of the same name. But while some dismiss tales of wildmen as fairy stories, and others point to evidence that tribes of oversized humans really did once exist, could they still lurk out there somewhere?

EVIDENCE

GIANT BONES
Much of the 'evidence' for many giant traditions amounts to little more than misunderstood fossil bones and large ancient structures. But the remains of real people of large stature have also been found, including a tribe of Anglo-Saxon 'giants', an average of 2m (6ft 8in) tall, in North Yorkshire, England.

GREY MAN, GREEN MAN?
Some people have reported disturbing encounters with a being called the 'Big Grey Man' in Scotland's Cairngorm mountains. Elsewhere in Europe, there are many tales of 'green men' (right) that lurked in the depths of the wild woodland and were occasionally seen around the edge of villages. They are a popular feature of medieval art.

999790790.789.7

DISTRIBUTION

Giant hominids such as Bigfoot and the Yeti are found around the world, but northern Europe's wildmen seem closer in form to modern humans.

HABITAT: Wildmen are frequently associated with deep forests and remote wilderness areas.

DIET: The diet of Europe's wildmen and giants varies – some folktales depict them as monstrous cannibals while others appear to eat an omnivorous diet of forest fruits and small animals.

TRACKS AND SIGNS

Modern accounts of encounters with wildmen often verge on the paranormal – creatures such as the Big Grey Man are said to create a paralysing fear in those they meet. Despite their size, these creatures come and go in silence and leave no trace.

POTENTIAL RISK: HIGH

The true intentions and intelligence of these creatures are unknown, but ancient traditions suggest they are best avoided.

SIZE COMPARISON

HEIGHT: 2.7m (9ft)
WEIGHT: 200kg (440lb)

PROXIMITY STATUS

WARNING: SUBJECT DISPLAYS SIGNS OF AGGRESSION – SEEK IMMEDIATE COVER

SIZE COMPARISON

WINGSPAN:
1.5m (5ft)
WEIGHT:
1.8kg (lb)

LEGENDS

THE CHINESE PHOENIX
The sacred bird of China is often called the Chinese phoenix, but its true name is the *fenghuang*, and it has little in common with the true phoenix of the Mediterranean region. According to tradition, it is the queen of the birds, a hybrid with the head of a pheasant, the body of a duck, the wings of a swallow and the tail of a pheasant. Although it does not go through the same cycle of life and death as the phoenix, the *fenghuang* is also associated with fire and the Sun. It is seen as a symbol of virtue and good luck, and was often used to represent the Chinese Empress, alongside the dragon as a symbol of the Emperor.

The ageing phoenix is said to build its nest and funeral pyre from twigs of myrrh, a resinous wood that was widely believed to have magical properties.

HISTORIC RECORD

c.800BC The Egyptian *Book of the Dead* refers to a phoenix-like bird called the *benu*.

1000BC

c.700BC Hesiod is the first to mention the phoenix by name, and to describe its long lifespan.

500BC

c.440BC Greek writer Herodotus describes the life cycle of the phoenix in his *Histories*.

0AD

c.170AD Flavius Philostratus writes his own account of the life cycle of the phoenix.

500AD

PRESENT DAY

39045675985509.098.08e83r93.00/43740.9-93776767------27896907
3r93.00/43740.9-93776767------278969074987.97979.08735

NORTHERN
EUROPE

Until the 19th century, northern Europe was a patchwork of deep
forests, farmland and isolated towns and villages huddling around
protective castles. Wild beasts such as wolves and bears lay in
wait for anyone who went astray, and there were countless other
creatures – supernatural beings that ranged from grumpy trolls
to mischievous fairies, from lake monsters to black dogs, and
from dragons to woodland giants. Even at home, you might not be
entirely safe – werewolves prowled on moonlit nights, and
vampires rose from their graves in search of human prey. Today
you're more likely to encounter a phantom cat than a black dog,
but the monsters of Europe still live on.

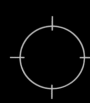

NORTHERN WILDMEN

All around the world, tales are told of encounters with enormous men, ferocious and possessed of immense strength. These giants are particularly common in the folklore of Scandinavian countries, where tales are often told of their battles with the old Norse Gods. Among the most famous is Grendel, a giant encountered by the hero Beowulf in the epic poem of the same name. But while some dismiss tales of wildmen as fairy stories, and others point to evidence that tribes of oversized humans really did once exist, could they still lurk out there somewhere?

EVIDENCE

GIANT BONES
Much of the 'evidence' for many giant traditions amounts to little more than misunderstood fossil bones and large ancient structures. But the remains of real people of large stature have also been found, including a tribe of Anglo-Saxon 'giants', an average of 2m (6ft 8in) tall, in North Yorkshire, England.

GREY MAN, GREEN MAN?
Some people have reported disturbing encounters with a being called the 'Big Grey Man' in Scotland's Cairngorm mountains. Elsewhere in Europe, there are many tales of 'green men' (right) that lurked in the depths of the wild woodland and were occasionally seen around the edge of villages. They are a popular feature of medieval art.

999790790.789.7

DISTRIBUTION

Giant hominids such as Bigfoot and the Yeti are found around the world, but northern Europe's wildmen seem closer in form to modern humans.

HABITAT: Wildmen are frequently associated with deep forests and remote wilderness areas.

DIET: The diet of Europe's wildmen and giants varies – some folktales depict them as monstrous cannibals while others appear to eat an omnivorous diet of forest fruits and small animals.

POTENTIAL RISK: HIGH

The true intentions and intelligence of these creatures are unknown, but ancient traditions suggest they are best avoided.

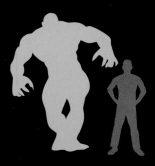

SIZE COMPARISON

HEIGHT: 2.7m (9ft)
WEIGHT: 200kg (440lb)

TRACKS AND SIGNS

Modern accounts of encounters with wildmen often verge on the paranormal – creatures such as the Big Grey Man are said to create a paralysing fear in those they meet. Despite their size, these creatures come and go in silence and leave no trace.

PROXIMITY STATUS

WARNING: SUBJECT DISPLAYS SIGNS OF AGGRESSION – SEEK IMMEDIATE COVER

HISTORIC RECORD

500AD

c.1140 Villagers at Woolpit in Suffolk, England, discover two strange 'green children'.

c.1600 A member of the Scottish Murray clan captures a wildman near Dundee. The family preserves an image of the creature on its coat of arms to this day.

1000AD

1925 Amateur climber Professor Norman Collie writes the first detailed description of an encounter with the Big Grey Man.

1500AD

1993 Hikers encounter a mysterious wildman-like creature in woodland near Aberdeen, Scotland.

2000AD

PRESENT DAY

OUT OF THE MISTS

Modern encounters with giants are often associated with horrific fear and supernatural abilities such as an ability to summon up dense fog out of nowhere. Some believe that such apparitions can be explained as 'waking nightmares', summoning up ancient fears of the extinct Neanderthal people of prehistoric Europe.

TROLLS AND OGRES

European folklore is full of tales of monstrous giants, trolls and ogres. Trolls come from the Scandinavian countries and are split into two breeds – large, hairy and barbaric monsters of the far north and smaller, more human-like creatures (often with tails) further to the south. The larger breed of troll is similar to the fearsome, sometimes man-eating, ogre of French, German and English fairy stories.

Trolls first appear in Viking epic poems or sagas from the 9th century. Rather like fairies and the djinns of Arabia (see p.16), they seem to be mostly invisible to humans, going about their own lives and only occasionally coming into contact with people. They are often seen as thieves, stealing crops, livestock and other supplies from remote farmhouses, and hoarding treasure. But in most tales they are not truly wicked, simply living by a different set of rules and, like fairies, punishing humans who break those rules. Their other fairy-like habits include abducting people and sometimes stealing newborn babies to leave their own offspring (so-called 'changelings') in their place.

Trolls may have started out as 'hidden people' (*Huldufólk*) similar to fairies, but fairytales of the Middle Ages turned them into more ferocious and thoroughly wicked monsters, with a taste for human flesh. These later trolls are often indistinguishable from ogres found in Britain, France and Germany.

Although the word ogre was invented by poets in the 12th century, the first real ogres were monsters called Gog and Magog that lived in Cornwall, in the west of England, long before the first people arrived in the British Isles.

Ogres are usually portrayed as horrendous man-eating giants, slow-witted but sometimes with magical powers. The most famous of these traditional ogres is surely the one encountered by Puss in Boots, the feline hero of an old French fairy tale written down by Charles Perrault in the late 1600s. This monster lives in a castle, terrorizing the land for miles around, and has the power to transform himself into other animals. The cunning Puss tricks him into changing into a mouse and then eats the ogre while he is powerless.

In recent times, as fear of trolls and ogres has receded, stories such as *Shrek* have taught us to be more sympathetic to these strange giants. Although frequently bad-tempered and often difficult to understand, they may not be as terrible as the storytellers of the Middle Ages would have us believe.

EVIDENCE

TROLLS IN THE LANDSCAPE
Travel to Norway or Iceland today and the locals will happily point out the signs of trolls in the countryside. Some hills and rock formations are described as petrified trolls, perhaps turned to rock by exposure to daylight, while other strange hills are thought to be the homes of trolls. Like other magical creatures, trolls are often found near water crossings and of course are famous for lurking beneath bridges in fairytales. In Iceland especially, trolls and their cousins the elves are widely respected and considered as real, if invisible, neighbours. Building projects, for example, are sometimes altered to avoid harming the elves.

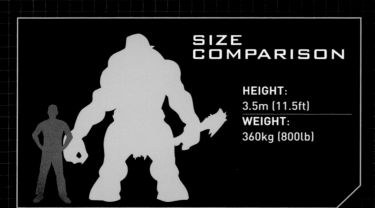

SIZE COMPARISON

HEIGHT:
3.5m (11.5ft)
WEIGHT:
360kg (800lb)

98509.098.08e83r93.00/43740.9-9377676------278969074987.97979.08735 2799

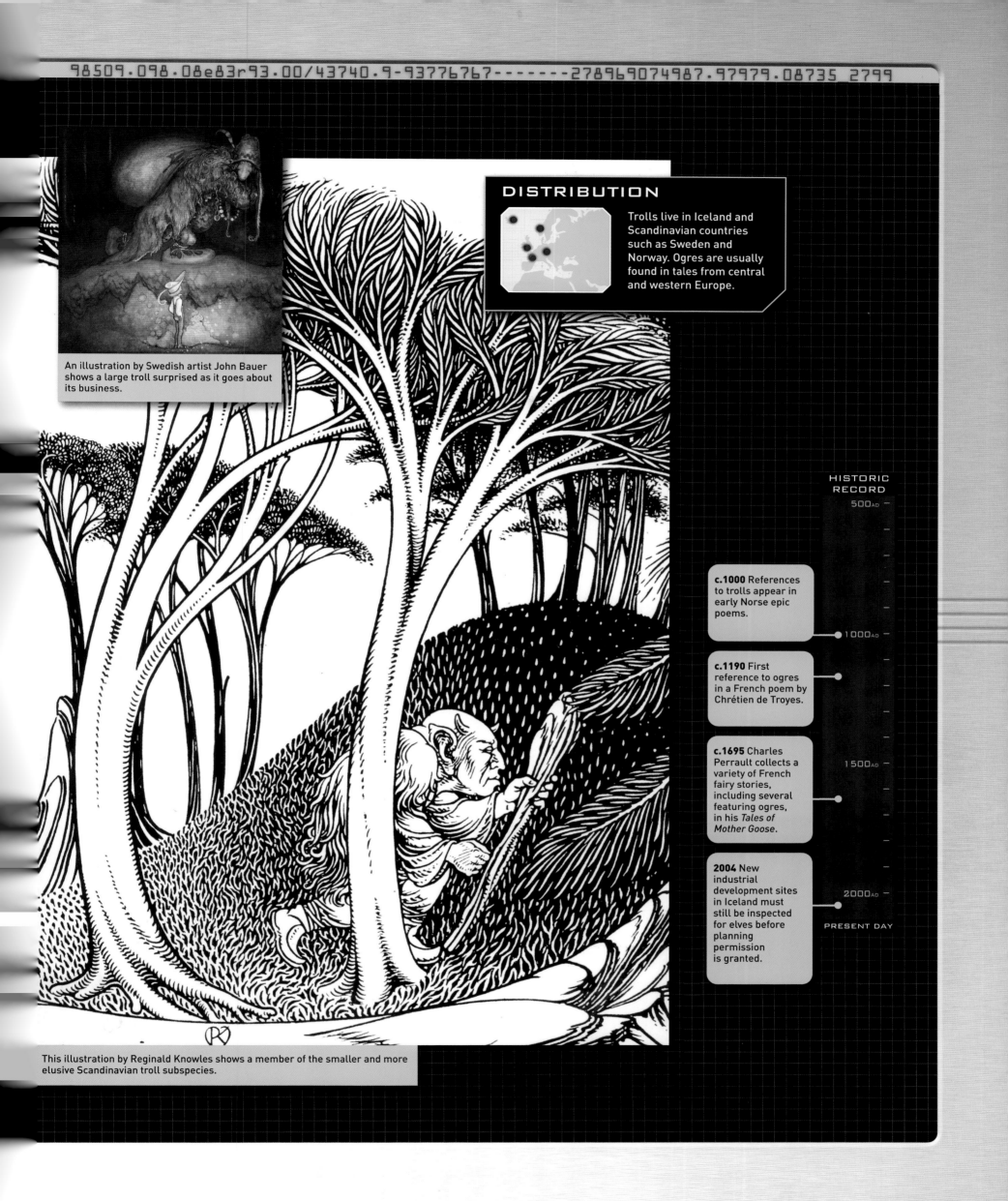

An illustration by Swedish artist John Bauer shows a large troll surprised as it goes about its business.

DISTRIBUTION

Trolls live in Iceland and Scandinavian countries such as Sweden and Norway. Ogres are usually found in tales from central and western Europe.

HISTORIC RECORD

500ᴀᴅ

c.1000 References to trolls appear in early Norse epic poems.

1000ᴀᴅ

c.1190 First reference to ogres in a French poem by Chrétien de Troyes.

c.1695 Charles Perrault collects a variety of French fairy stories, including several featuring ogres, in his *Tales of Mother Goose*.

1500ᴀᴅ

2004 New industrial development sites in Iceland must still be inspected for elves before planning permission is granted.

2000ᴀᴅ

PRESENT DAY

This illustration by Reginald Knowles shows a member of the smaller and more elusive Scandinavian troll subspecies.

47

DISTRIBUTION

Western dragons are largely associated with Europe, but have been seen as far afield as Africa and North America.

WESTERN DRAGON

Of all the world's fantastic creatures, the dragon is probably the most famous, and certainly the most majestic. It is found in two distinct subspecies – the ferocious, dinosaur-like western dragon and the more benign, serpent-like eastern or Chinese dragon. Western dragons are famed for a number of attributes, such as high intelligence (some have even been said to speak) and the ability to breathe fire. They also had a tendency, at least in medieval times, to hoard treasure and kidnap local maidens.

300

250

200

AUTO 150

100

50

0

FIRE BREATHERS

Some have speculated that dragons' stomachs have evolved to produce and store flammable methane gas, which they ignite with sparks from their teeth. But no one has got close enough to find out for certain!

PROXIMITY STATUS

WARNING: TAKE IMMEDIATE EVASIVE ACTION – EXTREME DANGER OF FIRE!

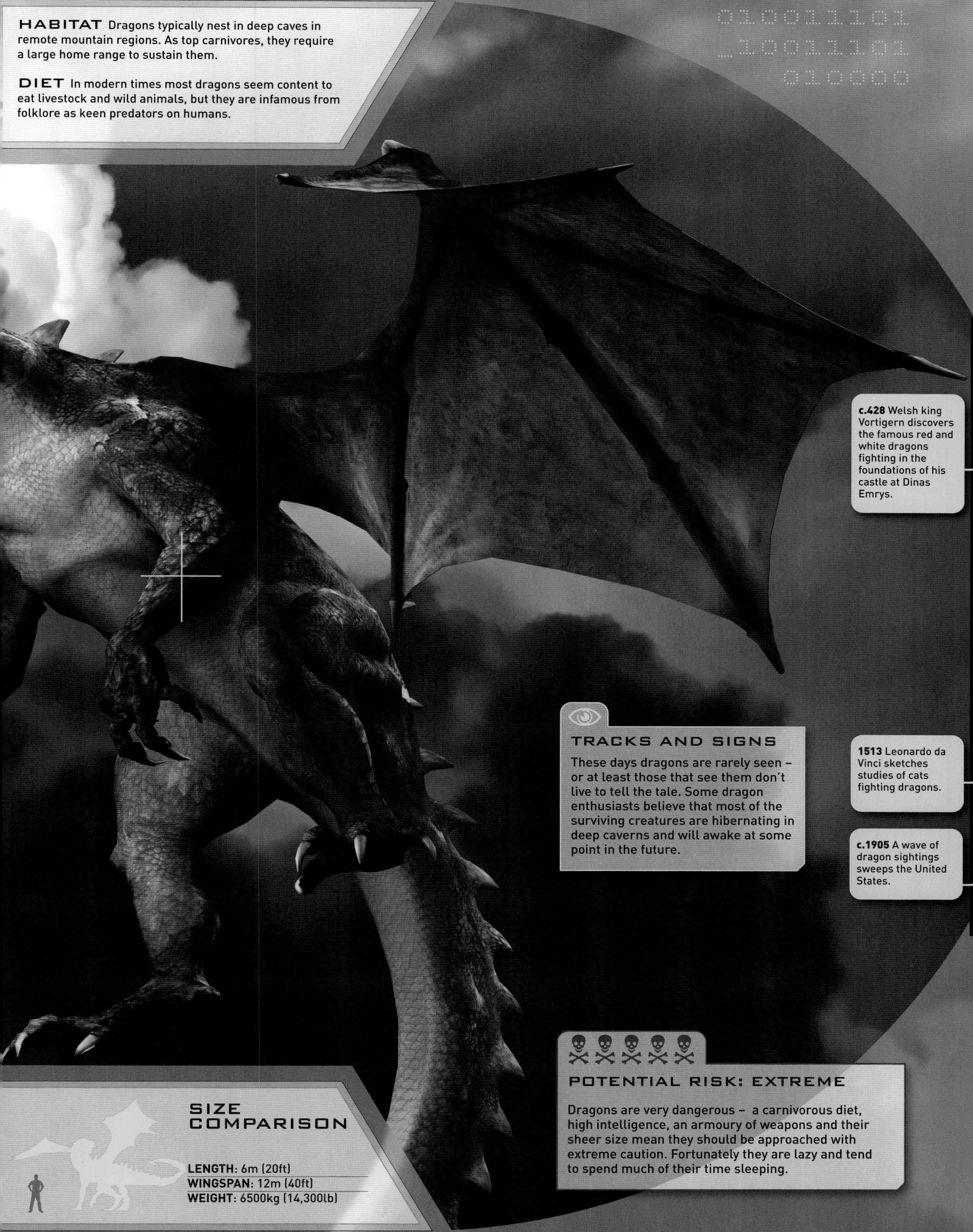

HABITAT Dragons typically nest in deep caves in remote mountain regions. As top carnivores, they require a large home range to sustain them.

DIET In modern times most dragons seem content to eat livestock and wild animals, but they are infamous from folklore as keen predators on humans.

010011101
_10011101
010000

HISTORIC RECORD

0AD

c.428 Welsh king Vortigern discovers the famous red and white dragons fighting in the foundations of his castle at Dinas Emrys.

500AD

1000AD

1500AD

1513 Leonardo da Vinci sketches studies of cats fighting dragons.

c.1905 A wave of dragon sightings sweeps the United States.

2000AD

PRESENT DAY

TRACKS AND SIGNS

These days dragons are rarely seen – or at least those that see them don't live to tell the tale. Some dragon enthusiasts believe that most of the surviving creatures are hibernating in deep caverns and will awake at some point in the future.

SIZE COMPARISON

LENGTH: 6m (20ft)
WINGSPAN: 12m (40ft)
WEIGHT: 6500kg (14,300lb)

POTENTIAL RISK: EXTREME

Dragons are very dangerous – a carnivorous diet, high intelligence, an armoury of weapons and their sheer size mean they should be approached with extreme caution. Fortunately they are lazy and tend to spend much of their time sleeping.

6360387-080-0.32786465849409-----999790790.789.7---8789468968940.0.0

THE WYVERN

A common mythical beast of northern Europe and particularly Britain, wyverns are dragon-like creatures with a few significant differences. Most obviously, they walk on two legs, and their wings are bat-like extensions from muscular arms, rather than additional limbs attached to the back as in four-legged dragons. Wyverns are generally less intelligent than true dragons, and they are unable to breathe fire, but some subspecies have the ability to exhale poison and all have sharp talons and a venomous stinging tail.

LEGENDS

DRAGON OR WYVERN?
In medieval times, the words dragon and wyvern were interchangeable. It was only in the 16th century that four-legged and two-legged beasts were given separate names.

THE MORDIFORD MONSTER
Perhaps the best known wyvern legend is the tale of the creature that terrorized the village of Mordiford in Herefordshire, England, after a local girl found it as a baby and raised it in secret. The monster was eventually defeated by a condemned criminal who was promised his freedom in exchange, but died from the influence of the wyvern's poisonous breath.

999790790.789.7

DISTRIBUTION

Unlike dragons, wyverns appear to be restricted to northwestern Europe and in particularly the western British Isles.

HABITAT: Like their larger relatives, wyverns favour remote areas with free-roaming livestock. They are also associated with rivers.

DIET: Wyverns are carnivorous, preying on animals ranging from rabbits and lambs to, in rare cases, cattle and even humans.

TRACKS AND SIGNS

The smaller size of wyverns allows them a wider range of roosting places than dragons, and although there is some evidence that they follow the same hunting routes from night to night, they do not necessarily adopt a single lair.

POTENTIAL RISK: HIGH

Fast-moving and agile predators, what wyverns lack in intelligence they make up for in instinct – approach with care!

SIZE COMPARISON

HEIGHT: 2.1m (7ft)
WINGSPAN: 4m (13ft)
WEIGHT: 130kg (290lb)

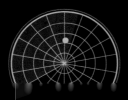

PROXIMITY STATUS

SUBJECT PREPARING FOR FLIGHT – MAINTAIN CAUTION

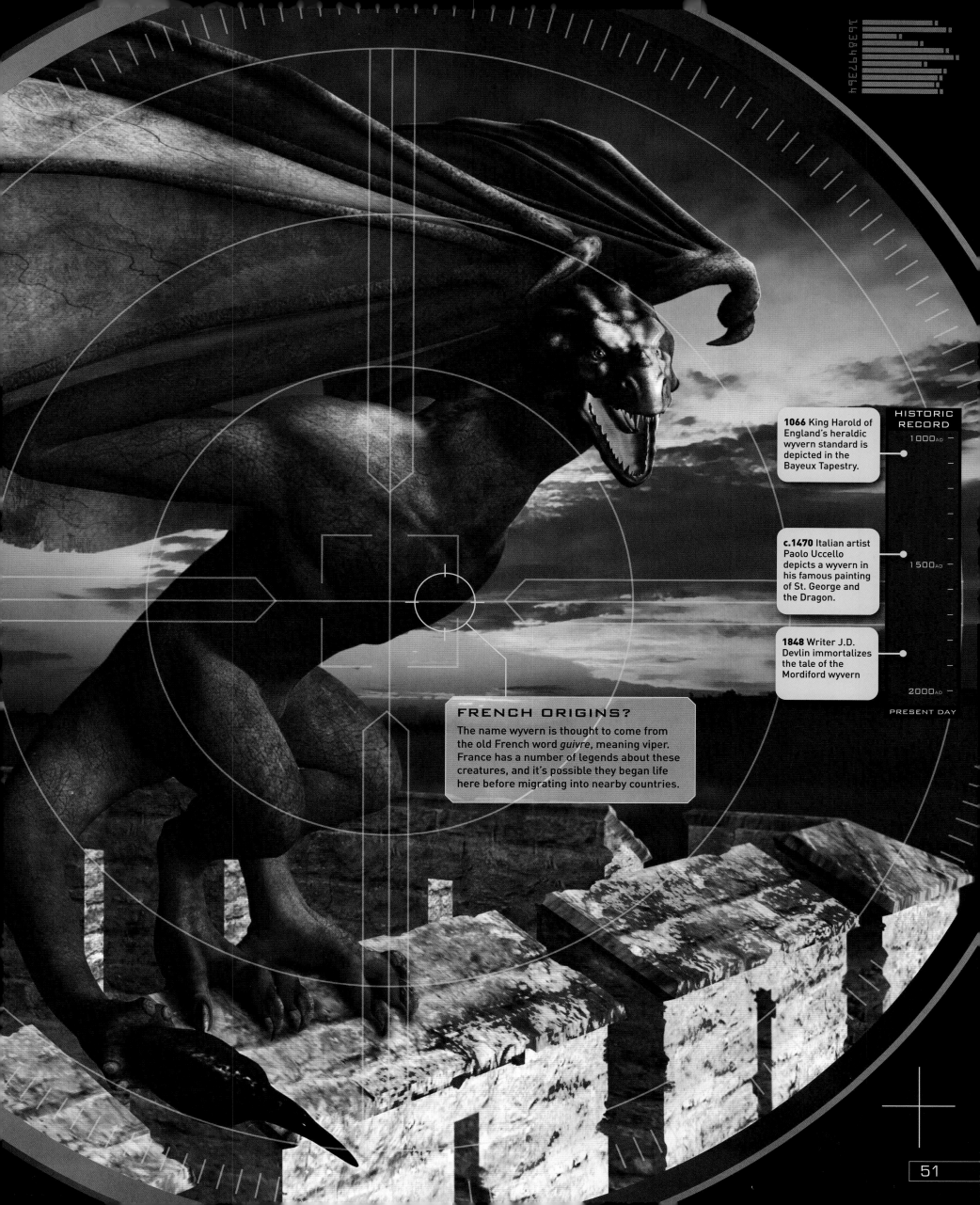

HISTORIC RECORD

1066 King Harold of England's heraldic wyvern standard is depicted in the Bayeux Tapestry.

1000AD

c.1470 Italian artist Paolo Uccello depicts a wyvern in his famous painting of St. George and the Dragon.

1500AD

1848 Writer J.D. Devlin immortalizes the tale of the Mordiford wyvern

2000AD

PRESENT DAY

FRENCH ORIGINS?

The name wyvern is thought to come from the old French word *guivre*, meaning viper. France has a number of legends about these creatures, and it's possible they began life here before migrating into nearby countries.

163904567598509.098.08e83r93.00/43740.9-93776767------278969074987.97979

SAINT GEORGE AND THE DRAGON

Perhaps the most famous dragon of all is the one fought by St. George. This tale is part of a long-running Christian tradition brought back to western Europe by knights returning from the Crusades and now attached to the popular saint.

The tale of Saint George and his battle with the dragon owes its present-day popularity to a medieval bestseller –*The Golden Legend*, compiled by Italian priest Jacobus de Voragine around 1260. This collection of biographies of saints, often wildly exaggerated and rich in fanciful tales from earlier writers, included a story of St. George that was already in wide circulation.

According to the legend, in the late 3rd century a poisonous dragon made its home at a large lake near the town of Silene in Libya, poisoning the waters and creating a famine that spread through the surrounding countryside. At first, the townspeople appeased the dragon by bringing it a sheep each day. But as the dragon's influence spread and the sheep stocks dwindled, they eventually made the terrible choice to offer it their children instead. Every day, lots were drawn and the children sent to the lake. Then one day the king's daughter was chosen. The king pleaded with his people, offering them his fortune if only they would spare the princess. But they would not accept and so the young maiden was sent to the lake.

It so happened that George, a Christian Roman soldier from Turkey, was riding past the lake and met the princess awaiting her fate. As the dragon emerged from the waters, the saintly soldier crossed himself and charged the beast with his lance, wounding it and restraining it with the help of the princess. The pair then led the dragon back to Silene, where George preached to them, offering to slay the dragon if the people would convert to Christianity. A healing spring supposedly emerged from the ground where the dragon died and a church was built on the spot.

As a late addition to the official life story of St. George, the tale of the dragon seems to have begun life independently. It shows a lot in common with other dragon legends – especially the story of Perseus and Andromeda (see Medusa, p.38). The main difference, of course, is that Perseus won the love of Andromeda, while St. George was doomed to die for his faith during the Emperor Diocletian's persecution of the Christians.

And what of the dragon itself? We really don't know enough from the story to judge what kind of dragon it was, but it shows a lot in common with the wingless subspecies known as wyrms (see over) – especially its affinity for water and its poisoning effect on the local water supply.

LEGENDS

ST. GEORGE IN ART
Ever since it was first told, the story of St. George and the dragon has inspired artists, poets and writers. The dragon has been depicted in many different forms – as a true dragon, a wyrm and a wyvern – and the story itself has been retold many times (sometimes even from the dragon's point of view!).

SAINTLY AFTERLIFE
The dragon legend has made St. George a uniquely valiant figure among saints, and many nations have adopted him as their patron saint. They include England, Greece, Aragon, Catalonia, Portugal and Russia, where a statue stands in Moscow (below).

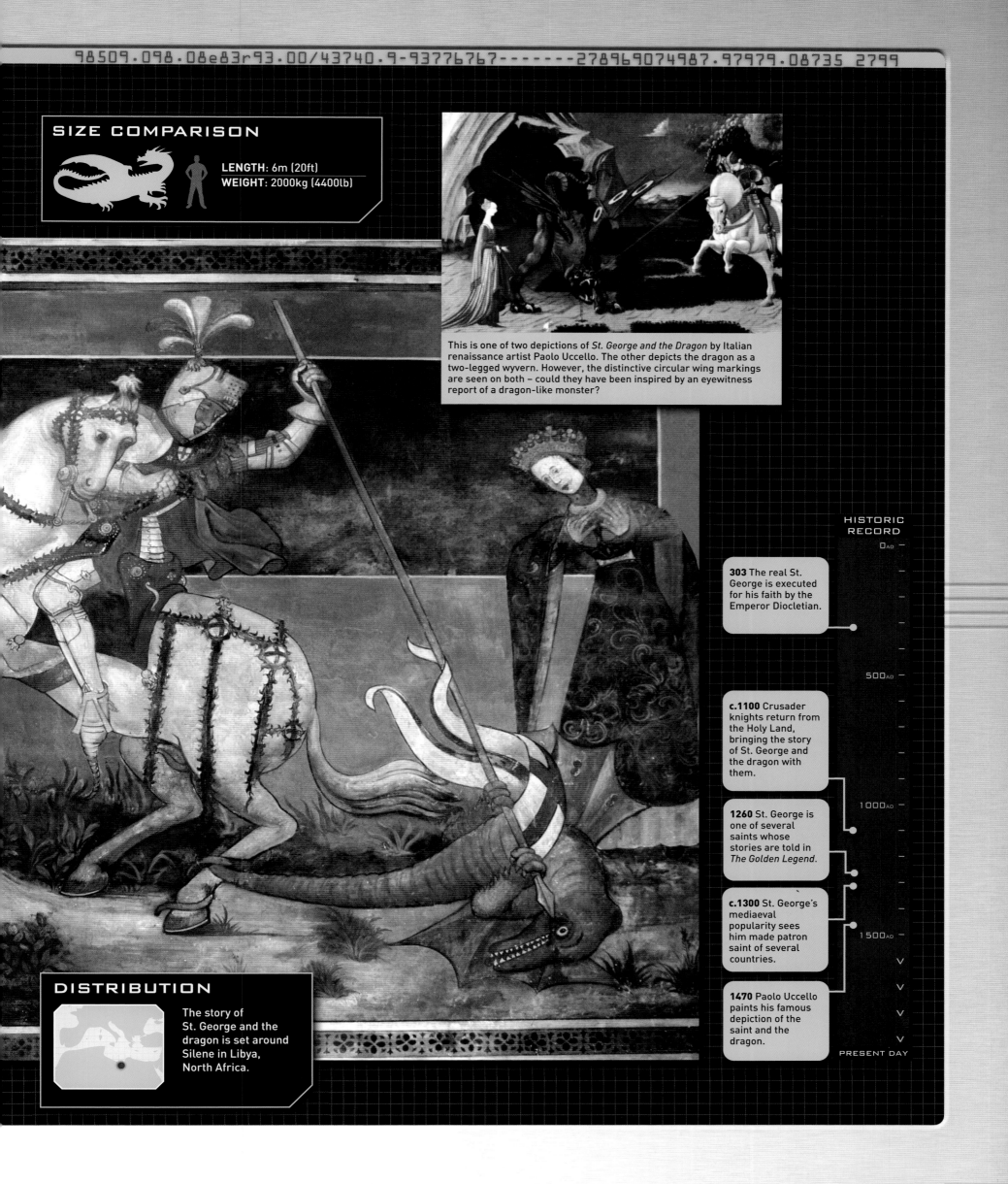

SIZE COMPARISON

LENGTH: 6m (20ft)
WEIGHT: 2000kg (4400lb)

This is one of two depictions of *St. George and the Dragon* by Italian renaissance artist Paolo Uccello. The other depicts the dragon as a two-legged wyvern. However, the distinctive circular wing markings are seen on both – could they have been inspired by an eyewitness report of a dragon-like monster?

DISTRIBUTION

The story of St. George and the dragon is set around Silene in Libya, North Africa.

HISTORIC RECORD

0AD

303 The real St. George is executed for his faith by the Emperor Diocletian.

500AD

c.1100 Crusader knights return from the Holy Land, bringing the story of St. George and the dragon with them.

1260 St. George is one of several saints whose stories are told in *The Golden Legend*.

1000AD

c.1300 St. George's mediaeval popularity sees him made patron saint of several countries.

1500AD

1470 Paolo Uccello paints his famous depiction of the saint and the dragon.

PRESENT DAY

DISTRIBUTION

Wyrm legends are common across northern Europe, but wyrms and dragons are often confused.

THE WYRM

Closely related to the majestic western dragon, but without the power of flight, wyrms are found across Europe, especially in Germanic and Scandinavian countries and the northern British Isles. Although four-legged like dragons, they lack the ability to breathe fire and instead produce noxious fumes. Often associated with rivers and wells, wyrms have an aquatic larval stage and never lose their liking for water. Although they appear to be widespread, the interchangeable use of the words 'wyrm' and 'dragon' in some countries can cause confusion.

300

250

200

AUTO 150

100

50

0

LEGENDS

THE LAMBTON WYRM

Several of the most famous wyrm legends come from northeastern England. The Lambton Wyrm story, for instance, tells the tale of John Lambton, a young and wayward heir to the local estate, who skips church one Sunday to go fishing. He catches a strange salamander-like creature and jokes that it is the devil itself before disposing of it down a local well. The creature's mere presence poisons the well. Years later it emerges as an enormous, fully grown monster that ravages the local livestock and is impervious to even serious wounds. When the grown-up John returns from the crusades as a gallant knight, he vows to defeat the wyrm. He eventually achieves this by covering himself in spiked armour, so that when the beast tries to crush him, it cuts itself to pieces.

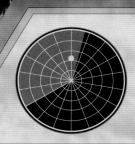

PROXIMITY STATUS

SUBJECT RESTING BUT VIGILANT – MAINTAIN SAFE DISTANCE

HABITAT
While dragons prefer to keep a distance from human habitation, wyrms are frequently found around the outskirts of civilization.

DIET
Wyrms are said to prey on livestock ranging from lambs to cattle, and occasionally on small children when they approach unwarily.

TRACKS AND SIGNS
Wyrms are most often found in their larval, water-borne form. Fully grown adults are rare these days, perhaps due to the increased management of water supplies – wyrms appear to prefer wells to waterworks!

SHAPESHIFTING WYRMS
Curiously, wyrms are often associated with tales of transformation. A typical example is 'The Laidley Worm of Spindlestonheugh', a Northumbrian folktale in which a king's daughter is turned into a wyrm by her wicked stepmother. The curse can only be broken by a kiss from her brother, who returns from overseas determined to kill the wyrm.

HISTORIC RECORD
500 AD

c.820 Renowned Viking warrior Ragnar Lodbrok wins fame by defeating a wyrm in Gotland, Sweden.

1000 AD

c.1000 The Scandinavian hero Beowulf's battle with a wyrm is recorded in an Old English epic poem.

1500 AD

c.1290 The Icelandic Volsunga saga tells the story of Fafnir, a greedy dwarf who turns into a wyrm in order to guard his hoard of gold better.

c.1300s Possible origins of the Lambton Wyrm story.

2000 AD

PRESENT DAY

POTENTIAL RISK: HIGH
While wyrms are not as mobile or well-armed as dragons, they are still fast-moving ground predators and should be approached with caution. Care should also be taken handling the larval forms, since these eel-like creatures already have a vicious bite.

SIZE COMPARISON

HEIGHT: 3m (10ft)
LENGTH: 8m (26ft)
WEIGHT: 4000kg (8800lb)

UNICORNS

Noble and elusive, the unicorn is perhaps the most beloved of all fabulous animals. Stories of these one-horned wonders are as old as history itself. Generally horse-like in appearance, they are distinguished from mundane horses not only by the long horn in the centre of their forehead, but also by their bearded chins and cloven hooves. Through various cultures, they have been seen as symbols of untameable strength, though without the savagery of more fearsome beasts.

EVIDENCE

UNICORN RECORDS
The earliest depictions of unicorns come from India's mysterious Indus Valley civilization, which flourished about 2500BC. They feature in the Bible, in oriental mythology, and in various Greek and Roman works of natural history.

HORNS AND SKELETONS
In medieval times, Europe had a lucrative trade in 'unicorn horns' from far northern shores. It was only as explorers ventured further north that it became clear these were in fact the tusks of narwhal whales. In 1663, German Otto von Guericke made a misguided attempt to reconstruct a unicorn skeleton from fossil mammoth and rhino bones.

999790790.789.7

DISTRIBUTION

Though elusive and rarely seen, unicorns are still thought to be widely scattered across Europe and much of Asia.

POTENTIAL RISK: MEDIUM
Although not openly aggressive, unicorns shun the company of humans and will lash out if cornered.

HABITAT Unicorns are mostly solitary animals of the deep forests. They do not seem to form herds, but come together only briefly to mate.

DIET Unicorns appear to feed on a variety of forest vegetation. Traditions say that herbs and forest barks allow them to live for several centuries.

TRACKS AND SIGNS
Unicorns are elusive and hard to track. However, their cloven hooves leave distinctive prints. According to tradition they can be lulled into a security by the presence of a beautiful maiden.

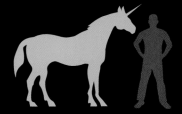

SIZE COMPARISON

HEIGHT: 2m (6.7ft)
LENGTH: 3m (10ft)
WEIGHT: 400kg (900lb)

PROXIMITY STATUS

SUBJECT PEACEFUL BUT WELL-ARMED AND EASILY STARTLED – AVOID SUDDEN MOVEMENTS

MAGICAL PROPERTIES

The unicorn's horn was supposed to have the ability to neutralise poison and instil other benefits. This encouraged the medieval trade in horns, and was bad news for the unicorn, but even worse for the narwhal.

HISTORIC RECORD

3000BC

c.2500BC Earliest unicorn images from the Indus Valley.

2000BC

1000BC

c.500BC Greek physician Ctesias describes the unicorn as an Indian animal.

0AD

1000AD

1298 Marco Polo mistakes the rhinoceros for a unicorn in the account of his travels.

2000AD

PRESENT DAY

163904567598509.098.08e83r93.00/43740.9-93776767------27896907
e83r93.00/43740.9-93776767------278969074987.97979.08735

THE TATZELWURM

A curious creature haunts the high pastures of the Swiss Alps, lying in wait for rabbits and unwary livestock. This is the *tatzelwurm*, a local form of dragon-like lizard that has the limbless hindquarters of a serpent, a single pair of strong forelimbs and a cat-like head. Despite its unusual shape, the *tatzelwurm* can leap over impressive distances to catch prey. Local farmers have known of its existence for centuries, but the animal's strange appearance leaves many cryptozoologists scratching their heads in search of explanations.

EVIDENCE

CONVINCED EXPERTS

During the 1930s, researchers collected evidence from some 60 witnesses. All agreed the *tatzelwurm* was no legend, but a flesh-and-blood animal. Several naturalists and other scientists have encountered the *tatzelwurm* face to face (right), but sightings have dwindled in recent years.

NOT-SO-LIMBLESS LIZARD?

One popular theory to explain the *tatzelwurm* is that it might be an unusual type of lizard called an amphisbaenid. These are superficially snake-like reptiles that have lost their limbs in order to burrow underground more efficiently. The *tatzelwurm*'s habit of burrowing certainly matches the description, but its huge size, aggressive nature and strong forelimbs certainly do not!

999790790.789.7

DISTRIBUTION

Known by several different names, the *tatzelwurm* is found across alpine Switzerland, Austria and southern Germany.

HABITAT *Tatzelwurms* appear to spend most of their time underground – they have often been disturbed while sleeping among the roots of trees.

DIET These strange creatures mostly eat small wild mammals such as rabbits, but will prey on unguarded livestock when the opportunity arises.

TRACKS AND SIGNS

One of the *tatzelwurm*'s alternative names translates as 'cave worm', and the best place to look for the animal is indeed in caves, hollows and other sheltered places. When lying still, it can easily be mistaken for a fallen branch or log.

POTENTIAL RISK: HIGH

There are several stories of *tatzelwurms* attacking unwary humans when disturbed, and local traditions say they breathe poisonous fumes.

SIZE COMPARISON

LENGTH: 3m (10ft)
WEIGHT: 100kg (220lb)

PROXIMITY STATUS

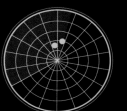

SUBJECT DISTRACTED BUT HIGHLY AGGRESSIVE – MAINTAIN SAFE DISTANCE

TOXIC ATTACKER

According to the detailed account of Joseph Scherer, who was attacked by a *tatzelwurm* in 1717, the evil-tempered creature was fairly easy to kill, but its toxic blood caused a severe swelling where it splashed his skin.

HISTORIC RECORD

1500AD
1600AD
1700AD
1800AD
1900AD
2000AD
PRESENT DAY

1717 Botanist Joseph Scherer and his son are attacked by a *tatzelwurm* while collecting herbs.

1828 A peasant finds a decaying *tatzelwurm* skeleton, and local experts fail to identify it. The remains are lost on their way to the University of Heidelburg.

1929 An Austrian schoolmaster encounters the *tatzelwurm* and is certain that it is some form of salamander.

1934 A Swiss photographer named Balkin takes what he claims is a photograph of the *tatzelwurm*, but many experts are unconvinced.

DISTRIBUTION

Greek writer Pliny the Elder put the first basilisks in North Africa, but the cockatrice's range seems to be confined to western Europe.

THE COCKATRICE

The cockatrice and its close relative, the wingless basilisk, are monstrous hybrids with a dragon-like body and the head of a rooster. Born from an egg laid by a cockerel and incubated by a toad, this animal is said to have the ability to turn those it meets to stone – either through its terrible gaze or with its poisonous breath. According to one legend, a cockatrice discovered beneath a chapel in Rome in the mid-9th century turned the air foul and killed many people. Most animals shy away from this freak of nature, but tiny weasels are immune to their powers and will attack them fearlessly. The cockatrice may eventually succumb to their vicious bites.

300

250

200

AUTO   150

➤

100

50

0

POOR FLYER

Although the cockatrice has dragon-like wings, they are quite small for its size, and the animal is only capable of awkward hopping flight.

TRACKS AND SIGNS

The only distinction between cockatrices and basilisks is the presence of wings on the cockatrice – otherwise the two animals have the same characteristics. Although it has a rooster-like call itself, the cockatrice will apparently die if it hears the crowing of a true cockerel.

POTENTIAL RISK: EXTREME

The cockatrice's deadly appearance makes it a fearsome killer, best avoided where possible. If confronted, be sure not to look directly into the beast's eyes. One tried and tested defence is to make the cockatrice look at its own reflection, so be sure to carry a mirror.

PROXIMITY STATUS

WARNING: SUBJECT CURIOUS AND AGGRESSIVE – AVOID GAZE AND RETREAT

HABITAT Incubated in moist conditions, cockatrices have a liking for cellars and crypts, particularly those beneath churches.

DIET Cockatrices are vicious meat eaters, prone to killing more than they can consume and partial to the flesh of all animals.

01001101
10011101
010000

500AD

850 A number of people in Rome die when a cockatrice beneath the Chapel of St Lucca poisons the air.

1180 English scholar Alexander of Neckam describes the cockatrice in a work on natural history.

1000AD

1538 Supposed date of the hatching of the Wherwell cockatrice.

1500AD

1733 A cockatrice emerges from the ruins of Renwick church in the English county of Cumbria during rebuilding.

2000AD

PRESENT DAY

LEGENDS

THE WHERWELL COCKATRICE

One of the the best-known cockatrice stories comes from Wherwell Priory in Hampshire, England. Here a cockatrice ran amok until it was imprisoned in the priory cellars. Several knights came to finish it off, but were killed by the ferocious beast. Finally a servant had the idea of lowering a mirror into the cellar. The cockatrice mistook the reflection for another of its kind, and fought the mirror tirelessly for hours on end. Finally, the servant lowered himself into the cellar and killed the exhausted monster with a spear.

SIZE COMPARISON

HEIGHT: 2.5m (8ft)
LENGTH: 3.5m (11.5ft)
WEIGHT: 300kg (600lb)

999790790.789.7

16390456759850⁹·098·08e83r93·00/43740·9-93776767------278969074987·97979

FAIRIES

The idea that there are creatures that move around us in an unseen realm and only occasionally connect with our own is an ancient one. In eastern traditions, the djinns fulfil this role, but Europe has the fairy folk – mischievous but powerful creatures with their own agendas, who live in a world of magic that obeys its own rules. People bargain with these elusive spirits at their peril.

The word fairy comes from the ancient name 'fae', meaning fate, but fairies are known by various other names. Some say they should never be referred to by their real name at all, preferring to call them 'the good folk', 'the fair folk' or one of several other complimentary nicknames.

The reason for this caution is that fairies have a dark side – occasionally playful but sometimes selfish and spiteful. Often they appear as the beautiful and delicate winged creatures seen in images such as the Cottingley fairy photographs. But other writers and artists, from William Shakespeare to Richard Dadd, have depicted them as more sinister and sometimes bizarre beings.

Those who deal with the fairies must follow strict rules – many fairy stories feature victims that break the laws of fairy generosity and suffer the consequences. In these cases, fairy gifts often have unpleasant consequences. For example, Thomas the Rhymer, a Scottish poet who rejected the Queen of Fairyland, found himself cursed with a tongue that would not lie.

Nothing about fairies is quite what it seems, thanks to their command of a kind of magic known as 'glamour'. When their spell is broken, fairy banquets are revealed to be weeds and fairy gold turns into rusty horseshoes.

A few people have also been guests in Fairyland itself, but these visits can also have unexpected results. Time seems to run differently in the fairy realm – there are tales of shepherds who spend what seemed like years in fabulous luxury, only to return home and find that mere minutes had passed. In contrast Herla, a king of the ancient Britons, feasted in Fairyland for three days and emerged to find England conquered, his kingdom gone and two centuries lost.

So what are the fairies? Some believe that they could be a 'race memory' – a distorted retelling of encounters between the Celtic people who spread across Europe in the first millennium BC and the earlier people who had shaped the landscape before them, putting up monuments that were often seen as the fairy castles and temples. Others have pointed out that old fairy stories have a lot in common with modern tales of alien encounters: perhaps fairies are aliens themselves, or supernatural creatures that have been seen in different forms in different ages. Or maybe they are simply what they appear to be – the little people who hide just out of sight and delight in making mischief.

EVIDENCE

THE COTTINGLEY FAIRIES
Perhaps the 'last gasps' of the original fairy tradition were the famous fairy photographs taken by young cousins Elsie Wright and Frances Griffiths near Bradford, England, in 1917. The photos caused an instant sensation. While many people said they were clever fakes, others (including Sherlock Holmes author Sir Arthur Conan Doyle) hailed them as proof of supernatural beings. Arguments about the nature of the pictures continued until 1981, when the cousins finally admitted faking most of them. However, they still insisted that their last photo was genuine, and that they had indeed seen real fairies.

98509.098.08e83r93.00/43740.9-93776767------27896907987.97979.08735 2799

SIZE COMPARISON

HEIGHT: 30cm (12in)
WEIGHT: Insubstantial

HISTORIC RECORD

1000ᴀᴅ

c.1150 Welsh historian Geoffrey of Monmouth writes of Morgan le Fay, a fairy enchantress at the court of King Arthur.

c.1250 Possible date of Thomas the Rhymer's encounter with the fairies.

c.1595 William Shakespeare depicts mischievous and sometimes sinister fairies in *A Midsummer Night's Dream*.

1500ᴀᴅ

c.1855–64 Artist Richard Dadd spends ten years in a mental hospital working on *The Fairy Feller's Masterstroke*.

1920 The Cottingley fairy photos are published, reigniting interest in fairies around the world.

2000ᴀᴅ

PRESENT DAY

Paintings of fairies were popular in Victorian England, and while most depicted fairies as beautiful, ghostly creatures, a few painters, such as Richard Dadd in *The Fairy Feller's Masterstroke*, saw their darker side.

DISTRIBUTION

Traditional fairies are widespread across Europe, but there are similar tales of magical hidden people around the world.

7926698·278921122·2·22·26782729290

DISTRIBUTION

Tales of mischievous spirits are common in folklore from around the world. Gremlins, however, have specific origins in 20th-century Britain.

GREMLINS, PIXIES AND SPRITES

The less attractive cousins of fairies, a variety of small creatures are said by folklore to revel in creating mischief and chaos. Pixies and sprites have a long history stretching back to medieval times, and delight in low-level trickery such as hiding precious items and leading travellers astray. Gremlins seem to be relatively new arrivals – fascinated by the machinery and electronics of the modern age, they take a particular interest in aircraft.

300 —

250 —

200 —

150 —
AUTO

➤

100 —

50 —

0 —

EVIDENCE

AIRCRAFT GREMLINS
During World War II, pilots in the Royal Air Force grew attached to the idea that mischievous creatures called gremlins were responsible for the inexplicable faults their aircraft occasionally developed. Ultimately they even adopted gremlins as mascots for their aircraft.

The idea of a new subspecies of fairy with a specific interest in mechanical mayhem rapidly caught on around the world, partly helped by the popularity of a story with the same name by the author Roald Dahl. The name may come from the Irish word *gruamain*, meaning a 'bad-tempered little person'.

TRACKS AND SIGNS

These beings rarely show their full physical form, though they sometimes appear as dancing orbs of light (so-called will o'the wisps). They can also become selectively visible to just a few people.

PROXIMITY STATUS

WARNING: IMMINENT SYSTEM FAILURE – REBOOT AND RETREAT!

999790790·789·7

16390456759850⁹·098·08e83r93·00/43740·9-93776767------278969074987·97979·08235

010011101
_10011101
010000

HABITAT Pixies and sprites are normally creatures of the countryside and tend to haunt lonely country lanes and isolated houses. Gremlins are attracted to all things technological, and are quite at home in modern cities.

DIET As supernatural creatures, these mischief-makers need no physical food.

GREMLIN GUISES

Simple creatures compared to the more sophisticated fairies, gremlins usually manifest themselves in a crude, unfinished form, looking like a fairytale goblin.

1900AD

1910AD

1922 Gremlins are first named, according to folklorist John Hazen.

1920AD

1929 First published mention of gremlins in a pilots' magazine.

1930AD

1940 Gremlins are 'adopted' by the air crews of the RAF's Photographic Reconnaissance Unit.

1940AD

1942 Roald Dahl, serving as an air attaché in Washington, writes a story that introduces the outside world to gremlins for the first time.

1950AD

PRESENT DAY

WREAKING HAVOC

It's possible that gremlins, like many other supernatural phenomena, have an associated electromagnetic field that could cause problems for delicate electronic instruments.

SIZE COMPARISON

HEIGHT: 30cm (12in)
WEIGHT: Insubstantial

☠☠☠☠☠

POTENTIAL RISK: MEDIUM

While these various spirits are incapable of directly inflicting harm on physical beings, their mischievous antics and particularly their fascination with machinery can lead to damaging consequences.

DISTRIBUTION

Although ghostly dogs are found around the world, the black dog tradition is particularly common in the British Isles.

BLACK DOGS

For centuries, certain areas of Britain have been haunted by legendary black dogs – canine spectres often seen as portents of death or associated with the devil. The most famous by far is the 'Hound of the Baskervilles'. It first appeared in a Sherlock Holmes story inspired by the legend of a huntsman on Dartmoor in southwest England, whose ghost supposedly rides with a pack of demonic hounds. Elsewhere, the black dog has a wide variety of names. In the east of England it is known as Black Shuck, in the north as the Barghest or Gytrash. But wherever they occur, these ghostly hounds strike fear into the hearts of those who encounter them.

300

250

200

TRACKS AND SIGNS

Black dogs are often seen before they are heard, either from a mournful howl or the padding sound of their footsteps. They instantly stand out from normal animals thanks to their glowing eyes and an ability to appear and disappear without warning.

AUTO 150

100

50

0

EVIDENCE

THE BLACK DOG OF BUNGAY
On 4 August 1577, Black Shuck made a terrifying appearance in the church at Bungay in Suffolk, later recorded in a pamphlet (right). While the congregation was saying Sunday prayers, a great storm broke around the church, the doors burst open and the monstrous black dog ran in, attacking at random and killing two people by breaking their necks. After terrorizing the church, Black Shuck disappeared as swiftly as he had come, reappearing later the same day at Blythburgh church, where scorch marks left on the door by his visit can still be seen to this day.

POTENTIAL RISK: HIGH

Although there are a handful of legends about friendly, harmless black dogs, most folklore agrees that they are dangerous creatures. Some, such as Black Shuck, inflict harm directly, but more often they are omens of doom, with repeated encounters indicating imminent death.

PROXIMITY STATUS

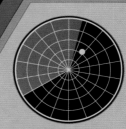

SUBJECT MATERIALIZING – REMAIN CALM AND RETREAT

999790790·789·7

HABITAT Black dogs, like many supernatural entities, are often found in association with streams, crossroads, ancient trackways and places of execution.

DIET Since black dogs are supernatural rather than physical creatures, they do not seem to require food. However, they may draw energy from the fear of those who see them.

01001110 1
_10011101
010000

KEEPING PACE

Many black dog reports involve the beast appearing alongside walkers on ancient country lanes at night. Some think that black dogs follow ancient 'ley lines' that run across the landscape and link places of mystical importance.

HISTORIC RECORD

1500 AD

1577 Black Shuck runs amok at the churches of Bungay and Blythburgh in Suffolk.

1600 AD

1677 Richard Cabell, Squire of Buckfastleigh on Dartmoor and inspiration for the wicked Sir Hugo Baskerville, dies and begins to haunt the moor with his ghostly hounds.

1700 AD

1893 At Rockland, Norfolk, two wagoners meet a black dog that explodes in a ball of fire when approached.

1800 AD

1901 Arthur Conan Doyle writes *The Hound of the Baskervilles*.

1900 AD

2000 AD

PRESENT DAY

SIZE COMPARISON

HEIGHT: 1.2m (4ft)
LENGTH: 1.8m (6ft)
WEIGHT: Insubstantial

6360387-080-0.3278646584940 9- - - - - -999790790-789-7- - -87894689689 40-0-0

VAMPIRES

Feared stalkers on the edges of civilization, vampires are humanoid creatures that feed on the blood of other living creatures. Some traditions say they are actually humans or the living dead. Although almost every ancient civilization has its own stories about vampiric beings, modern vampires spread from the Balkan area of southeastern Europe in the 18th century. Far from the romantic figures of gothic novels, true vampires are bestial, cadaverous creatures, driven by an insatiable need for blood. They are only deterred by various traditional protections including religious artefacts, plants including garlic, and the ultimate sanctions – beheading or a stake through the heart.

LEGENDS

THE REAL DRACULA
The most famous vampire of all is undoubtedly Dracula, depicted in Bram Stoker's novel of 1897 as a sophisticated nobleman from the Transylvania region of Romania. But the inspiration for Dracula was nothing like this urbane figure – Vlad III Dracula (right), who ruled much of Romania from 1456 to 1462, was a ruthless prince who executed thousands of political rivals and enemy soldiers by impaling them on spikes.

VAMPIRES AND BATS
Bram Stoker was also the first writer to link traditions of human vampires with the bloodsucking vampire bats that had been discovered in South America during the 1500s. However, the Maya people worshipped a giant bat god, Camazotz, and had their own vampire superstitions.

999790790.789.7

DISTRIBUTION

Traditions of vampire-like creatures are common around the world, from Eurasia to Africa, southeast Asia and the Americas.

HABITAT Vampires are usually depicted as haunting graveyards, rising from their coffins at night to go in search of prey.

DIET Vampires sustain themselves through absorbing life essence, usually in the form of blood. They may feed off a variety of animals, though they prefer humans.

TRACKS AND SIGNS
Vampires leave their victims with two distinctive puncture wounds from their fangs. They can take a variety of forms, and some can disguise themselves into more pleasing shapes, but all are revealed by their lack of reflection in a mirror.

POTENTIAL RISK: EXTREME
These vicious creatures are fast-moving and possessed of supernatural strength – vampire slayers beware!

SIZE COMPARISON

HEIGHT: c.170cm (5ft 8in)
WEIGHT: c.75kg (165lb)

PROXIMITY STATUS

WARNING: SUBJECT ALERT AND AGGRESSIVE – PREPARE DEFENSIVE TACTICS!

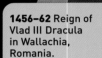

HISTORIC RECORD
1000AD

1456–62 Reign of Vlad III Dracula in Wallachia, Romania.

1721–34 A wave of vampiric attacks sweeps across central Europe, sparking mass panic.

1500AD

1819 John Polidori publishes *The Vampyre*, a gothic novel featuring the first 'modern' vampire, Lord Ruthven.

1897 Bram Stoker publishes *Dracula*.

2000AD

PRESENT DAY

VAMPIRE ORIGINS

The original Balkan vampires were identified when coffins were inspected and their corpses were found to be bloated – apparently a result of their nightly gorging on the blood of human and animal victims.

HOWLING AT THE MOON

Werewolves can be created in a number of different ways, including the bite of another werewolf, the wearing of magical animal skins or consumption of a specially prepared potion.

WEREWOLVES

Monstrous wolves are the stuff of mankind's worst nightmares – dangerous predators that would have hunted our ancestors as they spread around the world thousands of years ago. But are such wolves all that they seem? There are many reports of animals with enormous size, sometimes even walking on their hind feet in a human-like stance. Is it possible that some humans can actually transform into wolves of enormous strength and cunning? The idea of lycanthropy (from the Greek for 'wolf' and 'man') is found in folklore from all around the world and throughout history, but werewolf legends are particularly widespread in Europe.

HISTORIC RECORD

440BC Greek historian Herodotus writes of the Neuri, a tribe from the far north that are said to transform into wolves every nine years.

c.900 Norwegian king Harald I employs a retinue of Ulfhednar warriors, whose magical wolf-skin cloaks make them impervious to pain.

1764–67 Attacks by the 'Beast of Gévaudan' claim 100 French lives.

c.1810 The 'last werewolf' is supposedly killed near Morbach in Germany.

500BC

0AD

500AD

1000AD

1500AD

2000AD

PRESENT DAY

EVIDENCE

ONCE BITTEN?
The idea that a werewolf's bite can turn another person into a werewolf seems to be a quite recent invention. Earlier stories of werewolves suggest that they were the victims of curses or otherforms of witchcraft.

THE MORBACH MONSTER
German tradition states the last werewolf was killed at Morbach, near the southern city of Frankfurt. Supposedly he was a deserter from the French army, fleeing from Napoleon's ill-fated invasion of Russia in 1812. He was cursed after murdering an innocent farmer in his desperate search for food. After the beast was cornered and killed, a shrine was erected with a candle permanently burning to prevent its return. By 1988, this shrine lay on a US Air Force base. One night, a security patrol found the light had gone out. They joked about the monster, but later that night were alarmed by a huge, wolf-like intruder that terrified their dogs and cleared a high security fence in a single bound.

999790790.789.7

TRACKS AND SIGNS

Except when they move on two legs, werewolf tracks are indistinguishable from those of very large wolves. It is their fearlessness around humans that distinguishes them from their animal cousins and makes them far more dangerous.

SIZE COMPARISON

HEIGHT: 2.5m (8ft)
LENGTH: 2.5m (8ft)
WEIGHT: 150kg (380lb)

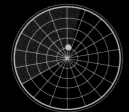

PROXIMITY STATUS

WARNING: SUBJECT HAS COMPLETED TRANSFORMATION – WITHDRAWAL RECOMMENDED

DISTRIBUTION

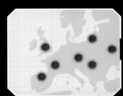

Werewolves of various types are found across Europe and Asia, wherever there were once native wolves They have also colonized the Americas.

HABITAT Werewolves live for most of the time unnoticed among human populations, only transforming into their monstrous form by the light of the full Moon. In human form, they are often unaware of their true nature, or deeply repentant of their attacks.

DIET Once transformed, a werewolf is overcome by insatiable bloodlust, killing anything it comes across.

POTENTIAL RISK: EXTREME

These deadly predators are averse to certain plants such as mistletoe and rye, and to the wood of the mountain ash. They can also be harmed by silver weapons.

16390456759850⁹.098.08e83r93.00/43740.9-93776767------27896907498⁷.97979

BEAST OF GÉVAUDAN

Between 1764 and 1767, the province of Gévaudan in central France lived in constant terror. A massive, wolf-like beast – or perhaps more than one – roamed the land, coming and going like a phantom while making attacks that were all too real. This mysterious monster killed perhaps 100 people throughout its rampage, and the deaths only came to an end after two separate animals were shot. Yet the Beast of Gévaudan's attacks are just the most infamous of many such incidents in French history.

The beast first emerged from the deep Gévaudan forests in early June 1764. A woman working on a farm at Langogne was the first to report it, when a large wolf-like animal charged at her from nearby woods, only to be driven off by her cattle. Within weeks, though, the beast had tasted blood, killing another woman at the nearby village of Les Hubacs.

From this time on, the animal's attacks became more frequent and bloody. Soon news of the *Bête Anthropophage du Gévaudan* (man-eating beast of Gévaudan) had spread across France. The death toll mounted rapidly, but in January 1765, a young boy called

Jacques Portefaix, together with six friends, successfully managed to fend off an attack by the beast. Word of their bravery reached the Royal Court of Louis XV and the king himself ordered that the children should be rewarded. Concerned that panic was spreading and the people were blaming his own government for allowing the beast to roam free, Louis also sent a pair of professional wolf-hunters to the region.

Despite several wolves being killed, the attacks continued. In June the king ordered the hunters to be replaced by François Antoine, his own master huntsman. In September 1765 Antoine shot a large grey wolf that several witnesses identified as the attacker, and for a time the attacks ceased. Antoine was hailed as a hero and showered with rewards and titles, but that was not the end of the story.

That December, two children were seriously injured at La Besseyre-Saint Mary, and the attacks resumed with renewed ferocity, killing dozens more. By this time, the interest of the Royal Court had moved on, and so the beast was allowed to run rampant until June 1767, when local hunter Jean Chastel shot and killed another huge wolf-like creature – some say using a silver bullet. When the beast was split open, human remains were found in its stomach. The beast's reign of terror, it seemed, was finally at an end.

The attacks around Gévaudan were not the first or last such incidents in France, but they were by far the worst and longest-lasting. Wolf attacks were more frequent in earlier times, when wolves themselves were more common and firearms had not yet taught them to fear humans. However, many people insisted the Beast of Gévaudan was no ordinary wolf, arguing that it was, at the least, an animal completely unknown to them, or perhaps even a supernatural creature.

EVIDENCE

WHAT WAS THE BEAST?
The creature shot by François Antoine was almost certainly a large wolf, or perhaps a wolf-dog hybrid. Many people saw it when it was stuffed and displayed in the king's palace at Versailles (below), and apart from its size, no one suggested there was anything unusual about it. But this beast was not responsible alone for the killings in Gévaudan, and the second monster is more of a mystery. Descriptions included a powerful tail and hoof-like claws, as well as small, round and distinctly un-wolflike ears. Suggested identities have included a hyena, a deformed bear, an escaped lion or even a werewolf.

98509.098.08e83r93.00/43740.9-9377676?------27896074987.97979.08735 2799

DISTRIBUTION

The beast was confined to Gévaudan, a small and mountainous region of south-central France.

SIZE COMPARISON

LENGTH: 3m (10ft)
WEIGHT: 200kg (440lb)

A popular illustration of the time dramatizes the moment when Jacques Portefaix and a small group of children fended off an attack by the beast.

HISTORIC RECORD

June 1764 First attacks in Gévaudan attributed to the beast.

January 1765 Hunters are despatched to the region to kill the beast.

September 1765 François Antoine kills the first beast and the killings temporarily come to a halt.

December 1765 The beast's killings resume.

June 1767 The second beast is killed, bringing an end to the terror.

1764 AD
1765 AD
1766 AD
1767 AD
1768 AD

PRESENT DAY

THE LOCH NESS MONSTER

Locals and visitors have reported occasional sightings of an enormous, long-necked creature in Scotland's largest lake for centuries. 'Nessie' – as it is affectionately known – has become one of the world's most famous mystery beasts. The monster has eluded a number of scientific expeditions sent to solve the mystery, and several infamous hoaxes have only confused matters further – most eyewitnesses cannot even agree on what kind of animal Nessie is!

300 —
250 —
200 —
AUTO 150 —
100 —
50 —
0 —

EVIDENCE

EARLY SIGHTING
According to the 7th-century *Life of Saint Columba*, the saint encountered a 'water beast' on the River Ness in the late 6th century. The first modern sighting was on 22 July 1933, when tourist George Spicer and his wife saw a long-necked creature crossing the road alongside Loch Ness.

THE SURGEON'S PHOTOGRAPH
The most famous image of the monster is now widely agreed to be a fake. The 'surgeon's photograph' (right), supposedly taken by a London doctor in 1934, actually shows a sculpted monster's head attached to a toy submarine.

999790790·789·7

TRACKS AND SIGNS

Most encounters with Nessie are brief glimpses of a humped shape moving through the still waters of the loch, leaving a wake behind it. It's rare to see the creature's head and neck above the water.

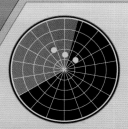

PROXIMITY STATUS

WARNING: SUBJECT BREACHING SURFACE – EVASIVE ACTION REQUIRED!

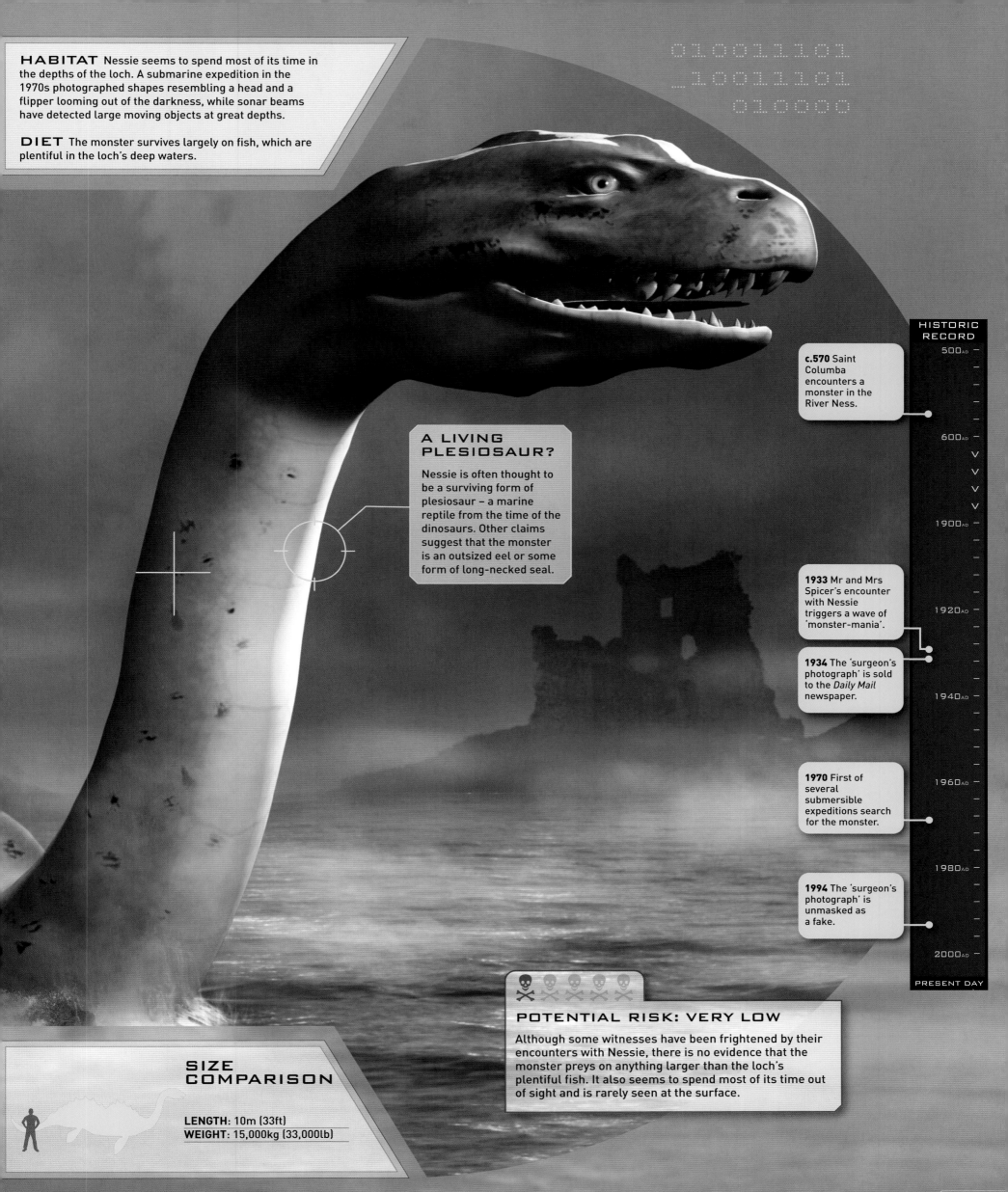

HABITAT Nessie seems to spend most of its time in the depths of the loch. A submarine expedition in the 1970s photographed shapes resembling a head and a flipper looming out of the darkness, while sonar beams have detected large moving objects at great depths.

DIET The monster survives largely on fish, which are plentiful in the loch's deep waters.

A LIVING PLESIOSAUR?

Nessie is often thought to be a surviving form of plesiosaur – a marine reptile from the time of the dinosaurs. Other claims suggest that the monster is an outsized eel or some form of long-necked seal.

500AD

c.570 Saint Columba encounters a monster in the River Ness.

600AD

1900AD

1933 Mr and Mrs Spicer's encounter with Nessie triggers a wave of 'monster-mania'.

1920AD

1934 The 'surgeon's photograph' is sold to the *Daily Mail* newspaper.

1940AD

1970 First of several submersible expeditions search for the monster.

1960AD

1980AD

1994 The 'surgeon's photograph' is unmasked as a fake.

2000AD

PRESENT DAY

POTENTIAL RISK: VERY LOW

Although some witnesses have been frightened by their encounters with Nessie, there is no evidence that the monster preys on anything larger than the loch's plentiful fish. It also seems to spend most of its time out of sight and is rarely seen at the surface.

SIZE COMPARISON

LENGTH: 10m (33ft)
WEIGHT: 15,000kg (33,000lb)

16390456759850°.098.08e83r93.00/43740.9-93776767------27896907
e83r93.00/43740.9-93776767------278969074987.97979.08735

PHANTOM CATS

Officially, the British Isles only have one wild species of cat – a wildcat slightly larger than a domestic tabby. Yet every year, dozens of people report seeing much larger animals, ranging in size from pumas to panthers. Some claim they are responsible for the mutilated livestock that are regularly found by farmers in remote parts of the country. Are these all mistaken sightings of domestic cats, or do giant felines really roam the British countryside? And if so, are they recent escapees from captivity, or something more ancient?

EVIDENCE

THE CATH PALUG
The lack of reported big cat sightings before the mid-20th century is often seen as evidence that phantom cats are recent escapees. But medieval Welsh legends tell the tale of a monstrous cat, the *Cath Palug*, that ran amok on the Isle of Anglesey. Some experts argue that 'black dog' legends (see p.66) may also be misinterpreted sightings of big cats.

THE BEAST OF EXMOOR
Perhaps the most famous phantom cat has been seen on Exmoor in Devon since the 1970s. It became notorious in 1983 after more than 100 sheep were found with their throats torn out over just three months. Royal Marine snipers staked out the area without success. Officials ultimately concluded the beast did not exist, despite continued sightings and photographs (right).

999790790.789.7

DISTRIBUTION

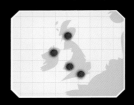

Sightings of out-of-place animals are reported from around the world, but inexplicable big cats seem to be a mainly British phenomenon.

HABITAT In general, phantom cats prefer remote wilderness and moorland, but they occasionally stray closer to human settlements.

DIET Despite the apparent size of the British phantom cat population, kills on livestock are quite rare, so it seems these animals can normally sustain themselves on small wild animals such as rabbits.

TRACKS AND SIGNS

These cats are generally silent and stealthy predators that disappear almost as soon as they are spotted. But they often leave footprints behind them, and have been heard to give screaming calls at night. They also leave unique marks on their prey.

POTENTIAL RISK: LOW

Although there are rare stories of cats lashing out when cornered, they generally flee when confronted by humans at close quarters.

SIZE COMPARISON

HEIGHT: 0.7m (2ft)
LENGTH: 1.8m (6ft)
WEIGHT: 90kg (200lb)

PROXIMITY STATUS

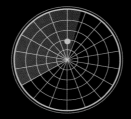

WARNING: SUBJECT SURPRISED AND AGGRESSIVE – AVOID SUDDEN MOVEMENTS

16390456759850°.098.08e83r93.00/43740.9-93776767------278969074987.97979.08735

ANCIENT OR MODERN?

Although many people attribute big cat sightings to animals released after a change in the laws about keeping wild animals in the 1970s, continued sightings today suggest the phantom cats have formed breeding populations around the British Isles. So could they actually be an ancient native species that has remained largely hidden?

HISTORIC RECORD

1950ᴀᴅ

1959 First sightings of the so-called 'Surrey Puma' in southern England.

1960ᴀᴅ

1970ᴀᴅ

1983 Sheep killings on Exmoor spark a wave of interest in the 'beast'.

1980ᴀᴅ

1991 A Eurasian lynx kills 15 sheep in Norfolk before it is shot.

1993 First sightings of a lion-like animal near the town of Basingstoke.

1990ᴀᴅ

1995 A leopard skull found on Bodmin Moor in Cornwall proves to be a hoax.

2000ᴀᴅ

PRESENT DAY

1639045675985097.098.08e83r93.00/43740.9-93776767------27896907

e83r93.00/43740.9-93776767------278969074987.97979.08735

THE AMERICAS

Native Americans have many tales of legendary beasts, but in the vast continents of North and South America, we cannot be so sure that most are supernatural. Many witnesses continue to see enormous creatures such as the thunderbird and Bigfoot (the *sasquatch*) to this day. Giant snakes of fearsome size may still lie in wait for unwary explorers in the Amazon jungles, and the Americas still regularly give rise to reports of new monsters such as the terrifying Mothman and the mysterious *chupacabras*, or goatsucker. Perhaps even modern encounters with aliens are in reality some new form of monster emerging from the darkness?

DISTRIBUTION

Usually associated with northwestern North America, Bigfoot-like creatures are sometimes seen in other parts of the United States.

BIGFOOT

North America's most famous mystery animal, Bigfoot is a giant ape-like creature that haunts the remote forests of the Pacific northwest and is sometimes seen much farther afield. This towering, shaggy-haired beast generally shuns the presence of people, but has been recorded in the stories of American Indian tribes since long before European settlers arrived. It has several names in native languages, but probably the most familiar is *sasquatch*. Numerous prints from its huge feet have been recovered and there have been many eyewitness encounters – but Bigfoot also seems to be uniquely popular among hoaxers trying to make a fast buck.

EVIDENCE

EARLY TALES

In the 1920s, Canadian author J.W. Burns collected traditions of wildmen from various Native American tribes and suggested that they were evidence of a real animal. He called it by its Halkomelem Indian name *sasquatch*.

FIRST FLAP

The name 'Bigfoot' was coined in 1958 when road builders near Bluff Creek in Humboldt County, California, found a series of huge footprints up to 40cm (16in) long. However, there is now good evidence that these prints were faked.

PATTERSON-GIMLIN FILM

The most famous images of Bigfoot were shot near Bluff Creek in 1967 by Roger Patterson and Robert Gimlin. They purport to show a large female Bigfoot, but sceptics say it is just a man in an ape suit. One man has even come forward to admit he was in the costume, though others doubt his claims.

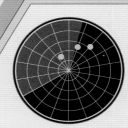

PROXIMITY STATUS

FAMILY GROUP RETREATING – MAINTAIN POSITION AND OBSERVE

300
250
200
AUTO 150
100
50
0

HABITAT Bigfoot favours extensive temperate rainforests remote from human habitation.

DIET Bigfoot is thought to live largely on nuts, berries and other forest vegetation, but has also been known to carry off animals such as small deer, pigs and even a dog. Some have suggested that the ape supplements its diet with meat in early winter prior to hibernation.

HAIRY BEAST

Various hair samples, supposedly from Bigfoot, have been analysed with a variety of techniques, including DNA analysis. While it's impossible to directly prove that a hair comes from Bigfoot, some samples are certainly from primates and cannot be linked to any known species.

CALL OF THE WILD

Captured on tape, Bigfoot's calls – a guttural mix of chimp-like chatter and low moaning sounds – still send a chill down the spine. Even some experts on animal calls admit they cannot be fakes, so they are some of the strongest evidence that *something* is out there.

TRACKS AND SIGNS

Bigfoot's tracks are typically much larger than those of humans, but otherwise similar, with five toes and a spacing appropriate to the creature's enormous stature. Other prints, showing varying numbers of toes or other deformities, are more puzzling.

HISTORIC RECORD

1900ᴬ

1920s J.W. Burns collects native stories of the *sasquatch* in Canada.

1920ᴬ

1924 Canadian Albert Ostman is allegedly abducted by a family of *sasquatch*, escaping after six days.

1940ᴬᴰ

1958 Discovery of the Bluff Creek footprints sparks worldwide interest in Bigfoot.

1960ᴬᴰ

1967 Patterson and Gimlin capture Bigfoot on film at Bluff Creek.

1980ᴬᴰ

1992 Anthropologist Grover S. Krantz proposes that Bigfoot is a surviving species of the enormous ape *Gigantopithecus*.

2000ᴬᴰ

2008 Two Georgia men spark a media frenzy by claiming to have the frozen body of a Bigfoot, but are soon exposed as hoaxers.

PRESENT DAY

SIZE COMPARISON

HEIGHT: 2.5m (8ft)
WEIGHT: 180kg (400lb)

POTENTIAL RISK: LOW

Despite its size and intimidating appearance, Bigfoot tends to flee from people. It has been known to make violent threat displays and there are even stories of animals throwing rocks at anyone who strays too close. But there are no credible accounts of physical attacks.

DISTRIBUTION

The skunk ape is found across the southeastern United States, with sightings in Arkansas, Oklahoma and the Carolinas, but especially Florida.

SKUNK APE

Often described as 'Bigfoot's southern cousin', the skunk ape or swamp monkey is a human-like creature reported across the southeastern United States. It is especially common in the Florida Everglades. With a distinctive reddish pelt and upright walk, it also has an appalling smell, memorably described by one witness as resembling a 'skunk that just had a fight with a dumpster'. While the US Parks Service dismiss the story as a local legend, the local Miccosukee tribe of Native Americans insist the skunk ape is a real creature; they are backed up by a host of reliable eyewitnesses and some intriguing photographic evidence.

300

250

200

AUTO 150

100

50

0

EVIDENCE

NATIVE TRADITIONS
Miccosukee tribal traditions claim a long awareness of the skunk ape, which they call *Sha'a'wan Ok*i – literally 'big water raccoon'.

THE MYAKKA PHOTOS
Some of the most intriguing photographs of the skunk ape were sent anonymously to the Sarasota Sheriff's Department in 2000. An unidentified woman claimed to have photographed the ape (above) as it entered her back yard in nearby Myakka on several occasions. Despite numerous appeals, the witness has never come forward. Experts are still arguing over the authenticity of the pictures.

999790790.789.7

TRACKS AND SIGNS

The typical signs of a skunk ape are rather similar to those of Bigfoot – an unmistakable pungent smell and outsized footprints. While the creature is sometimes described as having glowing eyes, it's more likely they are just highly reflective.

POTENTIAL RISK: LOW

Although some of the Myakka photos appear to show an aggressive display by the skunk ape, this is probably intended to intimidate. There are no records of skunk ape attacks on humans, but apparent killings of pets show that this is not an entirely peaceful primate.

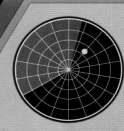

PROXIMITY STATUS

SUBJECT STATIC – DO NOT APPROACH AND MAINTAIN CAUTION

HABITAT Skunk apes have been seen in a variety of environments, but seem to favour humid swamplands such as the Florida Everglades.

DIET The skunk ape seems to be omnivorous. It generally sustains itself on vegetation including fruit stolen from gardens, but occasionally attacks animals.

ABOMINABLE STENCH

According to some skunk ape experts, the creature may live in abandoned alligator burrows deep in the Florida Everglades, absorbing the odour of decaying alligator kills into its pelt. This gives rise to its nauseating smell.

FOUR-TOED APE?

The numerous casts of skunk ape footprints are generally human-shaped, but typically around 35cm (14in) long. They seem to display just four toes on each foot.

SIZE COMPARISON

HEIGHT: 1.8m (6ft)
WEIGHT: 140kg (310lb)

HISTORIC RECORD

1940ad

1947 Earliest reported sighting in Lakeland, Florida.

1960ad

1975 Several sightings in Polk County, Florida, which rapidly becomes a focus for skunk ape reports.

1980ad

1997 Ochopee fire chief Vince Doerr spots a hairy man-like creature crossing the road near his home and manages to snap a blurry photo of the retreating beast.

2000ad

2000 The 'Myakka photographs' arrive at Sarasota Sheriff's Office. In following years, the area around Ochopee Lake becomes a hotbed of skunk ape sightings.

PRESENT DAY

16390456759B509.098.08e83r93.00/43740.9-9377676------278969074987.97979

THE JERSEY DEVIL

For more than two centuries, reliable witnesses have reported seeing a strange beast in the remote and swampy Pine Barrens wilderness of southern New Jersey. With bat-like wings and the head of a horse, this hoofed animal sounds at first like a modern equivalent of Pegasus – except that it preys on local livestock and has a terrifying scream. Most bizarrely of all, it also walks upright on its hind legs.

Perhaps unsurprisingly, given its curious appearance, this creature has become known as the Jersey Devil. The first reported sightings date to the early 19th century, when the creature was supposedly seen in separate incidents by US naval captain Stephen Decatur and Joseph Bonaparte, elder brother of French Emperor Napoleon I. These sightings may be local folklore in themselves, but repeated encounters with the strange creature certainly became common in the later 1800s, and a curious legend arose to explain them.

According to folklore, Deborah and Japhet Leeds had 12 children, after which 'Mother Leeds' jokingly swore that if she ever had another child, it would be the devil. But soon she fell pregnant again, and on a stormy night in 1735, she gave birth to her 13th child, a baby that instantly transformed into a winged demon. It struck the midwife dead and disappeared up the chimney, flying off in the direction of the Pine Barrens, where it presumably took a century to grow to adulthood.

From a local folktale, the Jersey Devil gained national notoriety in January 1909, when a wave of sightings made headline news across the United States. The towns of Burlington and Bristol, Pennsylvania, both awoke to find inexplicable 'devil's hoofprints' in the snow. Posses set off to hunt down the animal, though without success. This wave of activity culminated when the creature attacked a trolley car in the borough of Haddon Heights on 21 January. Throughout this week of panic, it was seen in various places often appearing to cross great distances more or less instantly. As armed guards were mounted, sightings of the creature became less frequent and eventually stopped completely.

Since then, the Jersey Devil has receded into folklore, although sightings continue to this day. Was it a demonic apparition? A series of mistaken sightings of normal animals that grew into a widespread panic? Or was it something more intriguing – a genuine unknown animal whose descendants might still lurk out of sight among the New Jersey Pine Barrens?

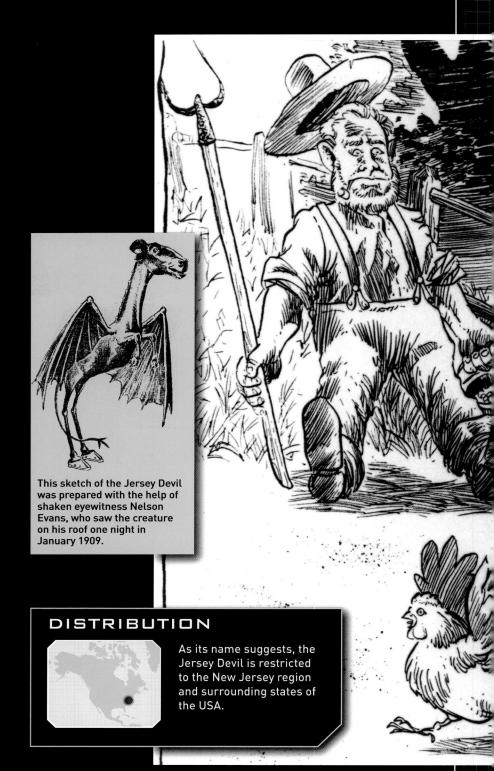

This sketch of the Jersey Devil was prepared with the help of shaken eyewitness Nelson Evans, who saw the creature on his roof one night in January 1909.

DISTRIBUTION

As its name suggests, the Jersey Devil is restricted to the New Jersey region and surrounding states of the USA.

98509.098.08e83r93.00/43740.9-93776767------278969074987.97979.08735 2799

EVIDENCE

DEVIL'S FOOTPRINTS
In 1855, large areas of the county of Devon in England experienced a similar panic to New Jersey after long lines of hoof prints were found in the snow one morning. Like the Jersey Devil's prints, they often ignored obstacles, crossing rooftops, fences and high walls without interruption.

AFRICAN DOUBLE
Some say that the bizarre-looking hammer-headed bat from the African rainforests (right) looks rather like the Jersey Devil – could a similar animal have somehow made it to New Jersey?

HISTORIC RECORD

1700ᴀᴅ

1735 Supposed birth of the Jersey Devil

c.1820 First sightings of the Jersey Devil.

1800ᴀᴅ

c.1840–1 First livestock killings are attributed to the creature.

1909 The Devil appears to dozens of people in New Jersey and neighbouring states over the course of a week or more.

1900ᴀᴅ

1960 Tradesmen in the town of Camden offer a $10,000 reward for the capture of the Devil.

2000ᴀᴅ

2007–8 A new wave of Devil sightings begin.

PRESENT DAY

SIZE COMPARISON

HEIGHT: 2m (6.7 ft)
WEIGHT: 120kg (260lb)

This humorous illustration from the 1909 wave of sightings shows a farmer surprised to find the Jersey Devil running amok in his chicken pen.

16390456759850·098·08e83r93·00/43740·9-93776767------27896907
e83r93·00/43740·9-93776767------278969074987·97979·08735

THE MOTHMAN

The infamous Virginia Mothman lingers somewhere between a real mystery creature and something less solid, yet more terrifying. It haunted the roads around Charleston and Point Pleasant for several months in 1966 and 1967, and its horrific appearance and glowing red eyes were reported by many reliable eyewitnesses. The apparitions came to an end around mid-December 1967, when the Silver Bridge at Point Pleasant collapsed and killed 46 people. But since then, the legend of the Mothman as a supernatural harbinger of disaster has grown in stature.

EVIDENCE

FIRST ENCOUNTER
The first people to report seeing the Mothman were two young couples driving past a disused explosives factory outside Point Pleasant on 15 November 1966. The first things they noticed were the creature's glowing red eyes. As it unfolded itself and revealed enormous bat-like wings, it took to the air, pursuing the car and its horrified occupants down Route 68 at speeds of up to 160 km/h (100 mph).

THE MOTHMAN PROPHECIES
As news of the Mothman spread, things got even stranger. Various people reported lights in the sky, mysterious phone calls and visits from intimidating, other-worldly 'men in black'. UFO researcher John Keel wrote a popular account of these events called *The Mothman Prophecies*.

999790790·789·7

November 1963
Reports of a Mothman-like creature around Hythe in Kent, England.

November 1966
First sightings of the Point Pleasant Mothman.

2 November 1967
Last accepted sighting of the Mothman, by four hunters in a park near Point Pleasant.

15 December 1967
Collapse of the Silver Bridge brings the original wave of sightings to an end.

1963 AD
1964 AD
1965 AD
1966 AD
1967 AD
1968 AD

PRESENT DAY

DISTRIBUTION

Since the original wave of sightings, similar creatures have been reported from as far afield as the United Kingdom and Mexico.

HABITAT Sightings of the Mothman and related creatures are often associated with water crossings.

DIET If the Mothman is a supernatural creature, it probably does not need to eat. But on the night of the first sighting, a dog disappeared from a nearby house. Something that looked like a dog's body was seen alongside Route 68, though later it could not be found.

TRACKS AND SIGNS
The Mothman's distinguishing features are its enormous red eyes, hunched appearance and huge bat-like wings. Some appearances were accompanied by a high-pitched screeching call.

POTENTIAL RISK: HIGH

While the Mothman has never directly attacked anyone, its terrifying appearance and association with imminent disaster make a sighting something to be feared rather than sought out.

SIZE COMPARISON

HEIGHT: 1.8m (6ft)
WINGSPAN: 4m (13ft)
WEIGHT: Insubstantial

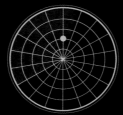

PROXIMITY STATUS

WARNING: SUBJECT APPROACHING RAPIDLY – REVERSE AND WITHDRAW IMMEDIATELY!

16390456759850·098·08e83r93·00/43740·9-93776767------278969074987·97979·08735

STUFF OF NIGHTMARES

According to *The Mothman Prophecies* author John Keel, the Point Pleasant creature is one manifestation of a paranormal 'window area' that can produce strange phenomena over long periods of time before returning to normal.

163904567598509.098.08e83r93.00/43740.9-93776767------278969074987.97979

LAKE MONSTERS

Although Scotland's Loch Ness Monster is probably the most famous 'lake monster', North America is home to countless similar creatures. They range from Ogopogo, the serpent-necked monster of Lake Okanagan in British Columbia, Canada, to the crocodile-like beast in Utah's Great Salt Lake and the flesh-eating octopus reported to live in Lake Thunderbird, Oklahoma. In fact, it sometimes seems as if every large body of water in North America has its own local monster.

Most of these lake monsters have only been reported since the mid-1800s as white settlers moved westward across America in greater numbers. But at least one of the most famous has a far longer history. Native Americans of the Iroquois and Abenaki tribes tell tales of a creature they call Tatoskok inhabiting Lake Champlain in upper New York State and this animal, better known by its modern nickname of 'Champ', has been seen by reputable witnesses for more than 100 years. The first reported sighting was by local sheriff Nathan H. Mooney in 1883. His description of a huge 'water serpent' in the lake encouraged others to come forward and admit they too had seen something strange in the lake. Circus owner P.T. Barnum was soon offering a $50,000 reward for the carcass of the Lake Champlain monster, but needless to say it was never claimed. However, the monster continues to be seen, and sometimes photographed, to this day.

Canada's Ogopogo, meanwhile, was first reported in 1872 by Susan Allison, a pioneer settler who also learned about it from native stories. It became front-page news in 1926 when dozens of people saw it from the shores of Lake Okanagan. In 1947 several people saw the creature up close from boats on the lake. One witness described a sinuous body about 9m (30ft) long, with five humps and a forked tail. Others saw a snake-like head with a blunt nose. Sightings of Ogopogo have continued to the present day and its name has been adapted for many other Canadian lake monsters, such as Manipogo of Lake Manitoba, and Winnipogo of Lake Winnipeg.

While descriptions of Champ and Ogopogo match the traditional view of lake monsters, many of the creatures reported from other lakes are unique. Lake Utopia in New Brunswick, for instance, sees regular reports of 'Old Ned', a whale-like beast with a large head. In the 1940s, Fulks Lake, Indiana, was the scene of a hunt for an enormous, livestock-eating snapping turtle known as Oscar. And a century earlier, several residents around the Great Salt Lake in Utah claimed to have seen a beast with the body of a crocodile and a horse-like head.

DISTRIBUTION

Lake monsters are found all around the world, but Canada and the United States seem to have by far the largest population and the greatest variety.

This 19th-century illustration depicts a close encounter with 'Old Ned', the monster of Lake Utopia, New Brunswick. Note the contrast between the creature's typical 'sea serpent' body and its bulky, whale-like head.

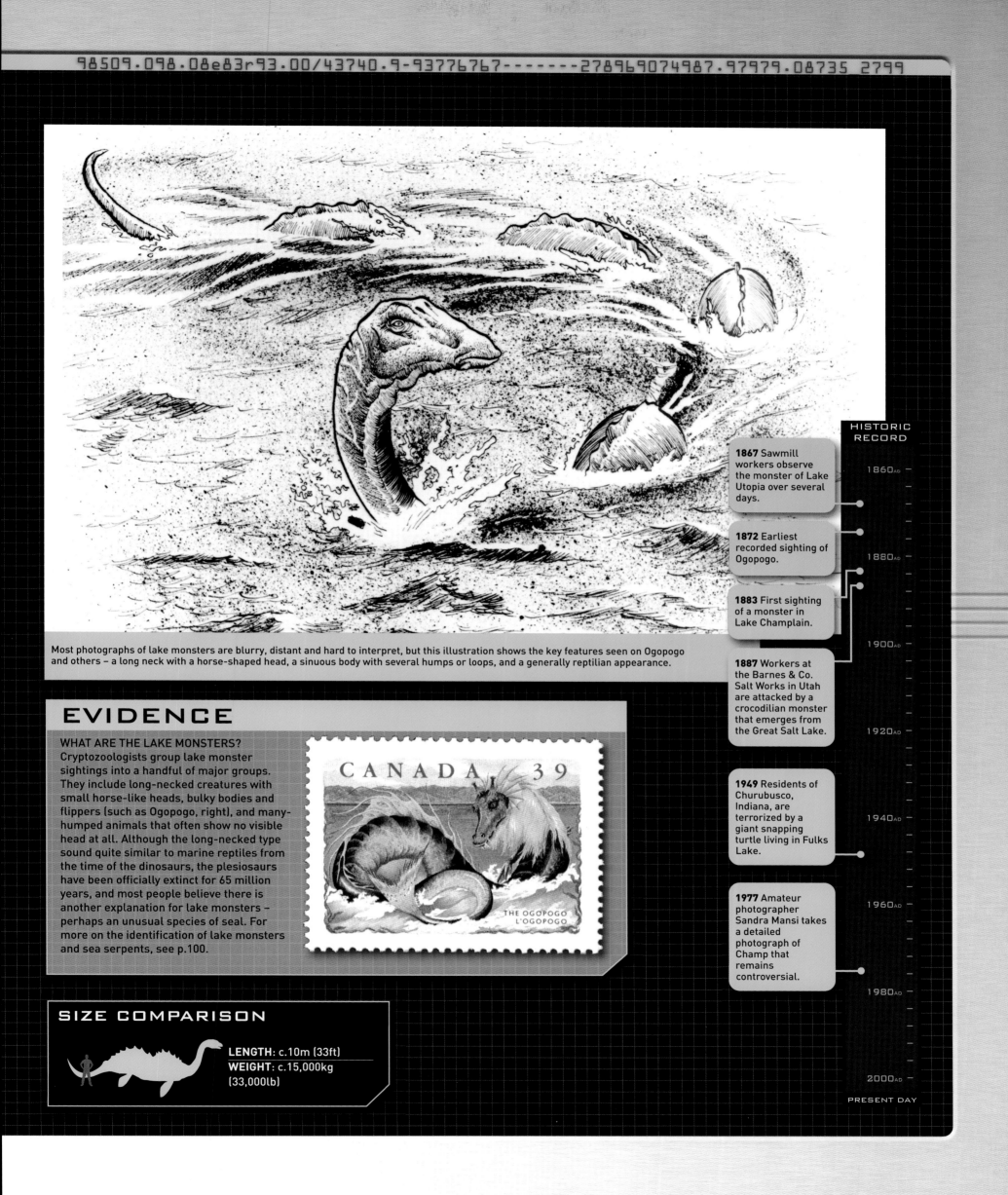

Most photographs of lake monsters are blurry, distant and hard to interpret, but this illustration shows the key features seen on Ogopogo and others – a long neck with a horse-shaped head, a sinuous body with several humps or loops, and a generally reptilian appearance.

EVIDENCE

WHAT ARE THE LAKE MONSTERS?
Cryptozoologists group lake monster sightings into a handful of major groups. They include long-necked creatures with small horse-like heads, bulky bodies and flippers (such as Ogopogo, right), and many-humped animals that often show no visible head at all. Although the long-necked type sound quite similar to marine reptiles from the time of the dinosaurs, the plesiosaurs have been officially extinct for 65 million years, and most people believe there is another explanation for lake monsters – perhaps an unusual species of seal. For more on the identification of lake monsters and sea serpents, see p.100.

CANADA 39

THE OGOPOGO
L'OGOPOGO

SIZE COMPARISON

LENGTH: c.10m (33ft)
WEIGHT: c.15,000kg (33,000lb)

HISTORIC RECORD

1860AD

1867 Sawmill workers observe the monster of Lake Utopia over several days.

1872 Earliest recorded sighting of Ogopogo.

1880AD

1883 First sighting of a monster in Lake Champlain.

1900AD

1887 Workers at the Barnes & Co. Salt Works in Utah are attacked by a crocodilian monster that emerges from the Great Salt Lake.

1920AD

1949 Residents of Churubusco, Indiana, are terrorized by a giant snapping turtle living in Fulks Lake.

1940AD

1977 Amateur photographer Sandra Mansi takes a detailed photograph of Champ that remains controversial.

1960AD

1980AD

2000AD

PRESENT DAY

7926698-278921122-2-22-26782729290

DISTRIBUTION

Thunderbirds range across the United States and into Mexico. Some believe the birds follow the same migration route each year.

THE THUNDERBIRD

Native American stories tell of an enormous bird whose beating wings create thunderclaps and whose appearance heralds the onset of the storm season. For years these tales were dismissed as mere folklore – no bird so big could possibly have flown in reality. But in 1980, fossil hunters in Argentina discovered the remains of a monstrous bird with a wingspan of 8m (26ft). *Argentavis magnificens* (the 'magnificent Argentine bird') was a teratorn, a vulture-like bird thought to have died out some 6 million years ago. But could the many thunderbird sightings be evidence that this monster bird has survived to the present day?

300 —
250 —
200 —

AUTO 150 —

TRACKS AND SIGNS

The thunderbird's association with storms may be more than folklore. Modern sightings seem to coincide with bad weather, and some researchers believe that these giant birds could ride the thermals in the same way as large eagles.

100 —

50 —

0 —

PROXIMITY STATUS

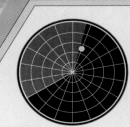

SUBJECT AIRBORNE AND GLIDING – MAINTAIN SAFE DISTANCE

163904567598509-098-09b6a940-93-00/93740-9-93776767- - - - -2789650749A7-52979-0873-

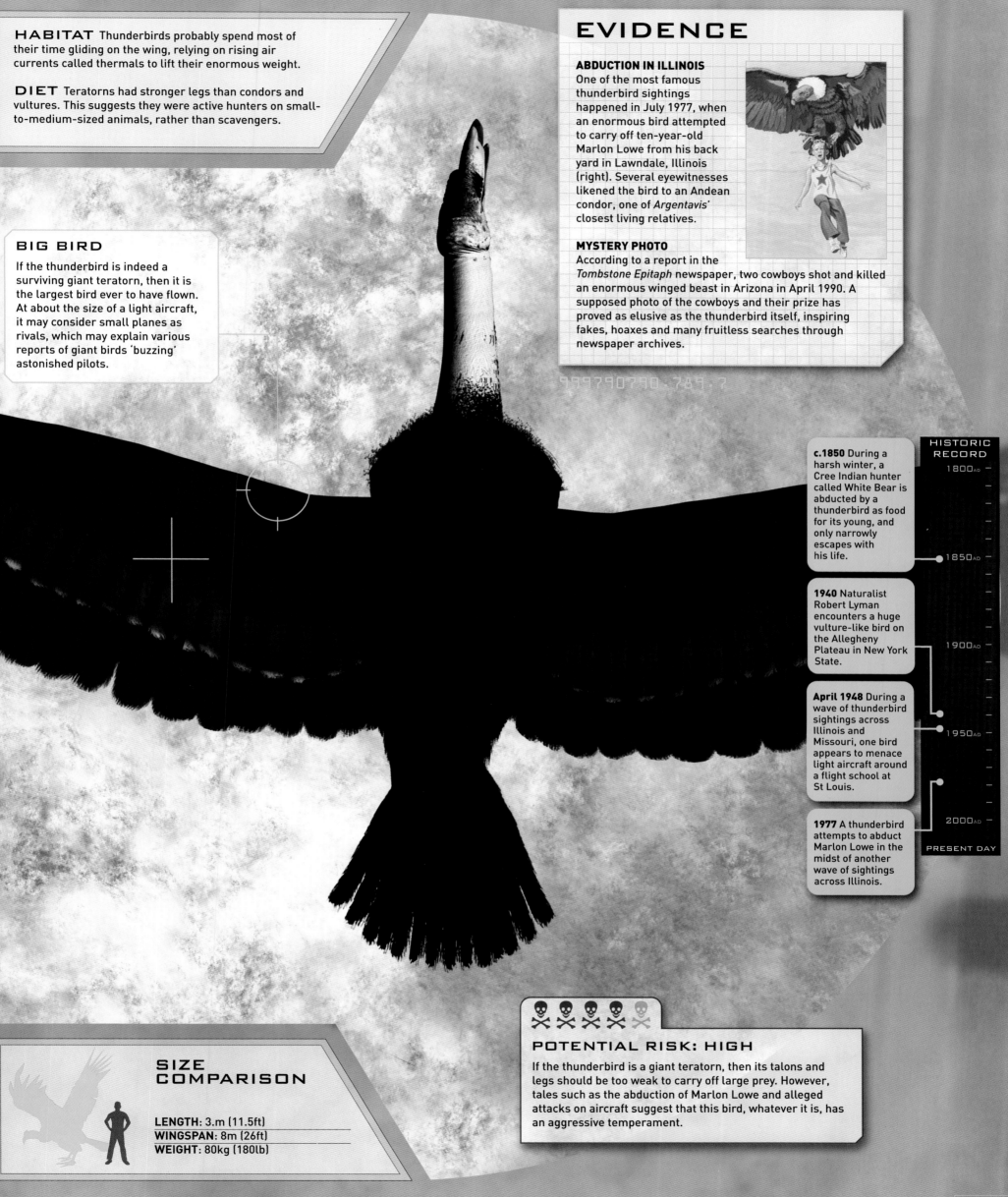

HABITAT Thunderbirds probably spend most of their time gliding on the wing, relying on rising air currents called thermals to lift their enormous weight.

DIET Teratorns had stronger legs than condors and vultures. This suggests they were active hunters on small-to-medium-sized animals, rather than scavengers.

BIG BIRD

If the thunderbird is indeed a surviving giant teratorn, then it is the largest bird ever to have flown. At about the size of a light aircraft, it may consider small planes as rivals, which may explain various reports of giant birds 'buzzing' astonished pilots.

EVIDENCE

ABDUCTION IN ILLINOIS
One of the most famous thunderbird sightings happened in July 1977, when an enormous bird attempted to carry off ten-year-old Marlon Lowe from his back yard in Lawndale, Illinois (right). Several eyewitnesses likened the bird to an Andean condor, one of *Argentavis'* closest living relatives.

MYSTERY PHOTO
According to a report in the *Tombstone Epitaph* newspaper, two cowboys shot and killed an enormous winged beast in Arizona in April 1990. A supposed photo of the cowboys and their prize has proved as elusive as the thunderbird itself, inspiring fakes, hoaxes and many fruitless searches through newspaper archives.

HISTORIC RECORD

1800ᴀᴅ

c.1850 During a harsh winter, a Cree Indian hunter called White Bear is abducted by a thunderbird as food for its young, and only narrowly escapes with his life.

1850ᴀᴅ

1940 Naturalist Robert Lyman encounters a huge vulture-like bird on the Allegheny Plateau in New York State.

1900ᴀᴅ

April 1948 During a wave of thunderbird sightings across Illinois and Missouri, one bird appears to menace light aircraft around a flight school at St Louis.

1950ᴀᴅ

1977 A thunderbird attempts to abduct Marlon Lowe in the midst of another wave of sightings across Illinois.

2000ᴀᴅ

PRESENT DAY

SIZE COMPARISON

LENGTH:	3.m (11.5ft)
WINGSPAN:	8m (26ft)
WEIGHT:	80kg (180lb)

POTENTIAL RISK: HIGH

If the thunderbird is a giant teratorn, then its talons and legs should be too weak to carry off large prey. However, tales such as the abduction of Marlon Lowe and alleged attacks on aircraft suggest that this bird, whatever it is, has an aggressive temperament.

EL CHUPACABRAS

Since 1995, a new mystery animal has made its presence felt across South America. Apparently originating in Puerto Rico, *el chupacabras* ('the goatsucker') kills its prey by draining the blood, leaving only three tell-tale puncture wounds in the chest. As news of the initial killings spread, so did eyewitness accounts of a strange reptilian beast with a kangaroo-like gait, glowing red eyes and a row of sharp spines running along its back. Today, the *chupacabras* seems to have spread across the continent, with sightings reported as far north as Texas and possibly beyond.

EVIDENCE

THE GOATSUCKER STRIKES

Early in 1995, eight sheep were found on a farm in Puerto Rico, drained of blood. Within months, 150 animals were dead around the town of Canovanas and people started to report sightings of a strange animal. Although the *chupacabras* appeared quite suddenly, some researchers link it to a spate of similar livestock killings in the 1970s.

TEXAN BEASTS

Since 2004, residents of Texas and elsewhere have photographed, and even shot and killed, strange hairless beasts whose appearance superficially matches descriptions of the goatsucker. DNA studies have shown that some of these animals are coyotes with a rare form of mange, but others seem to defy identification. One of the strangest features of the *chupacabras* is the huge variation in descriptions and drawings of the creature.

999790790.789.7

DISTRIBUTION

The *chupacabras* has spread from Puerto Rico to Mexico and Texas, with suspicious animal deaths reported as far afield as Chile and Maine.

HABITAT This strange creature seems to loiter near human habitation, especially where there are small livestock animals to be taken.

DIET The *chupacabras* feeds on a wide range of small-to-medium sized livestock, ranging from sheep and goats to chickens. However, it leaves the flesh untouched, drinking only the animals' blood.

TRACKS AND SIGNS

The *chupacabras* is said to have a distinctive screech, glowing red eyes and a sulphurous stench. Some eyewitnesses have reported a wave of nausea and fear, as though the animal has some sort of psychic defence mechanism.

POTENTIAL RISK: LOW

Although there is still a lot to learn about the *chupacabras*, there is little reason to believe it poses a direct threat to humans.

SIZE COMPARISON

HEIGHT: 1.2m (4ft)
WEIGHT: 50kg (110lb)

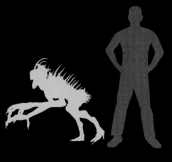

PROXIMITY STATUS

SUBJECT DISTRACTED AND UNAWARE OF NIGHT VISION APPARATUS – MAINTAIN OBSERVATION

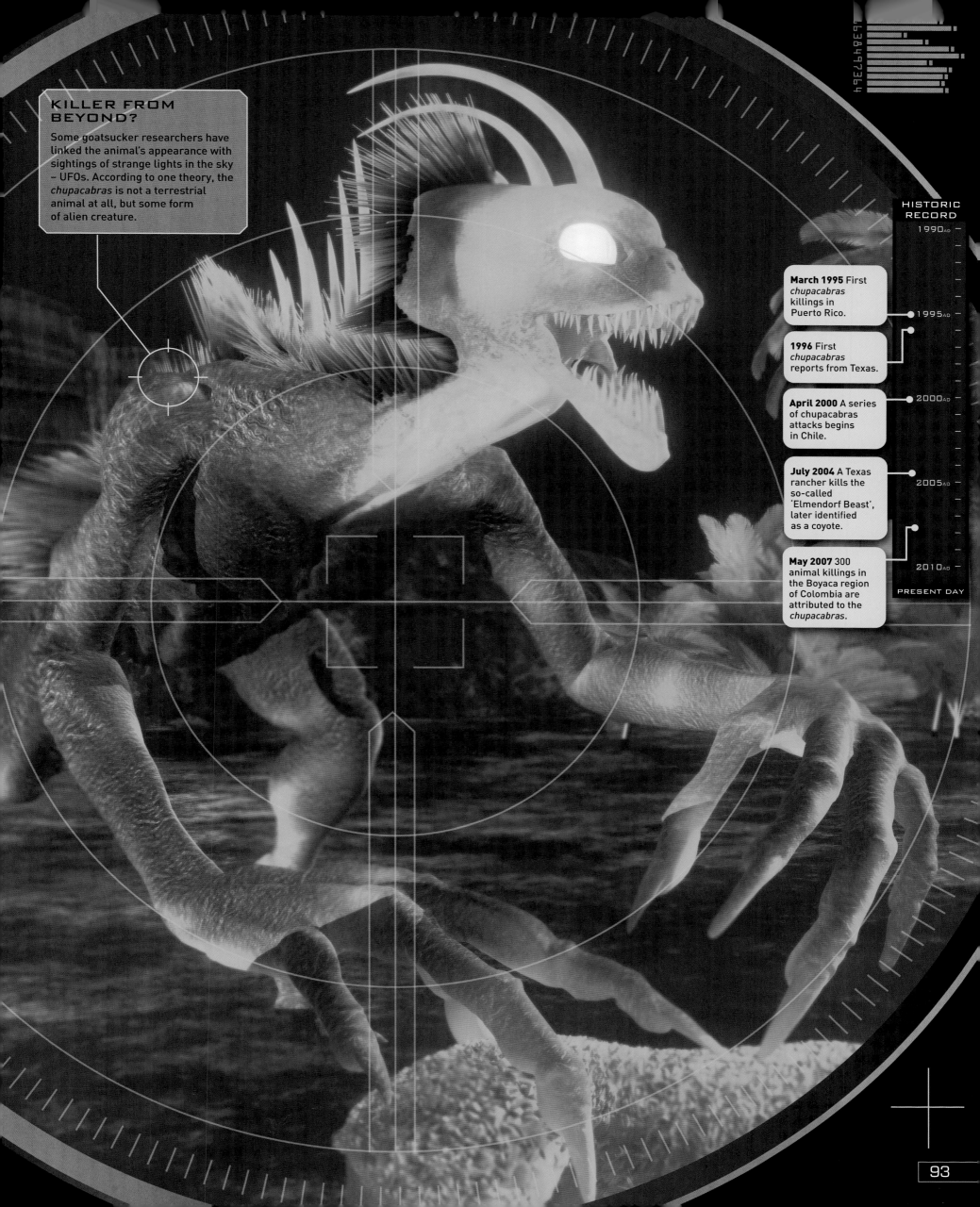

KILLER FROM BEYOND?

Some goatsucker researchers have linked the animal's appearance with sightings of strange lights in the sky – UFOs. According to one theory, the *chupacabras* is not a terrestrial animal at all, but some form of alien creature.

1990ᴀᴅ

March 1995 First *chupacabras* killings in Puerto Rico.

1995ᴀᴅ

1996 First *chupacabras* reports from Texas.

2000ᴀᴅ

April 2000 A series of chupacabras attacks begins in Chile.

July 2004 A Texas rancher kills the so-called 'Elmendorf Beast', later identified as a coyote.

2005ᴀᴅ

May 2007 300 animal killings in the Boyaca region of Colombia are attributed to the *chupacabras*.

2010ᴀᴅ

PRESENT DAY

16390456759850٩.09৪.08e83r93.00/43740.9-9377b7b7------278969074987.97979

GIANT ANACONDAS

Just how big do snakes get? According to scientists, the largest South American anacondas can grow up to 9m (30ft) long and can weigh as much as 250kg (550lb). These beasts can be large enough to swallow animals such as jaguars and caiman (medium-sized crocodiles), but explorers and natives alike have reported much larger serpents, some of truly enormous proportions.

Ever since the first European explorers ventured into the South American jungles in the 1500s, there have been reports of monstrous snakes from this remote part of the world. The natives call this great water-serpent the *sucuriju gigante*, while Spanish colonists knew it as *matora*, 'the bull eater'. While the accepted world record size for a snake (almost 9.9m or 33ft long) is held by a reticulated python from Celebes, Indonesia , these South American snakes, generally accepted as larger relatives of the green anaconda, can reportedly reach astounding lengths – perhaps growing to more than 30m (100ft). Anacondas are constrictors – snakes that kill their prey by wrapping around it and tightening their coils until the victim suffocates, after which they swallow it whole, dislocating their jaws if necessary. The thought of a snake capable of swallowing large cattle in this way is truly the stuff of nightmares.

British explorer Colonel Percy Fawcett encountered one such monster while surveying the borders of Brazil and Bolivia for the Royal Geographical Society around 1906. After shooting the creature dead, he was able to measure its length at 19m (62ft).

Fawcett's report was widely mocked by the scientific establishment when he returned to England, but that did not stop others from seeing giants snakes. Missionary Father Victor Heinz saw a live specimen, some 24.5m (80ft) long and as 'thick as an oil barrel' swimming in the Amazon in 1925. A few years later a French expedition shot and killed a specimen that they estimated at 23m (75ft) long.

It's understandable that scientists are sceptical about estimates of the length of snakes – especially when they are seen at a distance and coiled up or wrapped around branches. But the people involved in these encounters often had the opportunity to measure dead snakes laid out flat. There have also been several photographs of giant snakes, including one claimed to be 40m (131ft) long. But without conclusive proof of the scale of these pictures, the experts have remained cautious. The jungles of South America are so hostile and remote that it's little wonder no one has ever emerged dragging the remains of a giant snake. However, until someone brings back physical evidence, it seems that the *sucuriju gigante* will remain in the realms of cryptozoology.

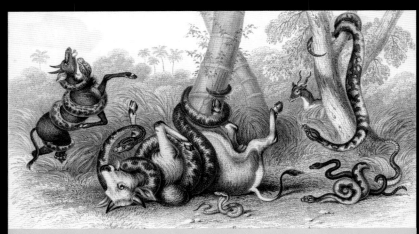

A 19th-century illustration shows a variety of snakes, of which the anaconda, depicted choking the life out of a large bull, is by far the most fearsome.

EVIDENCE

FURTHER AFIELD
Giant snakes are not entirely confined to the Amazon. In 1959 Belgian helicopter pilot Colonel Rene van Lierde photographed a snake some 12-15m (40-50ft) long in the Belgian Congo (now the Democratic Republic of Congo).

AN ANCIENT GIANT
In 2009, scientists unearthed the largest fossil snake so far discovered. Still shorter than some anaconda reports, *Titanoboa correjonensis* is a record breaker not just for its length of 12-15m (40-50ft), but also for its bulk, with a maximum diameter of 1m (40in) and a weight of

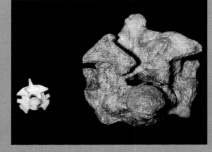

perhaps 1150kg (2500lb). The picture above shows a *Titanoboa* backbone alongside that of a normal modern anaconda.

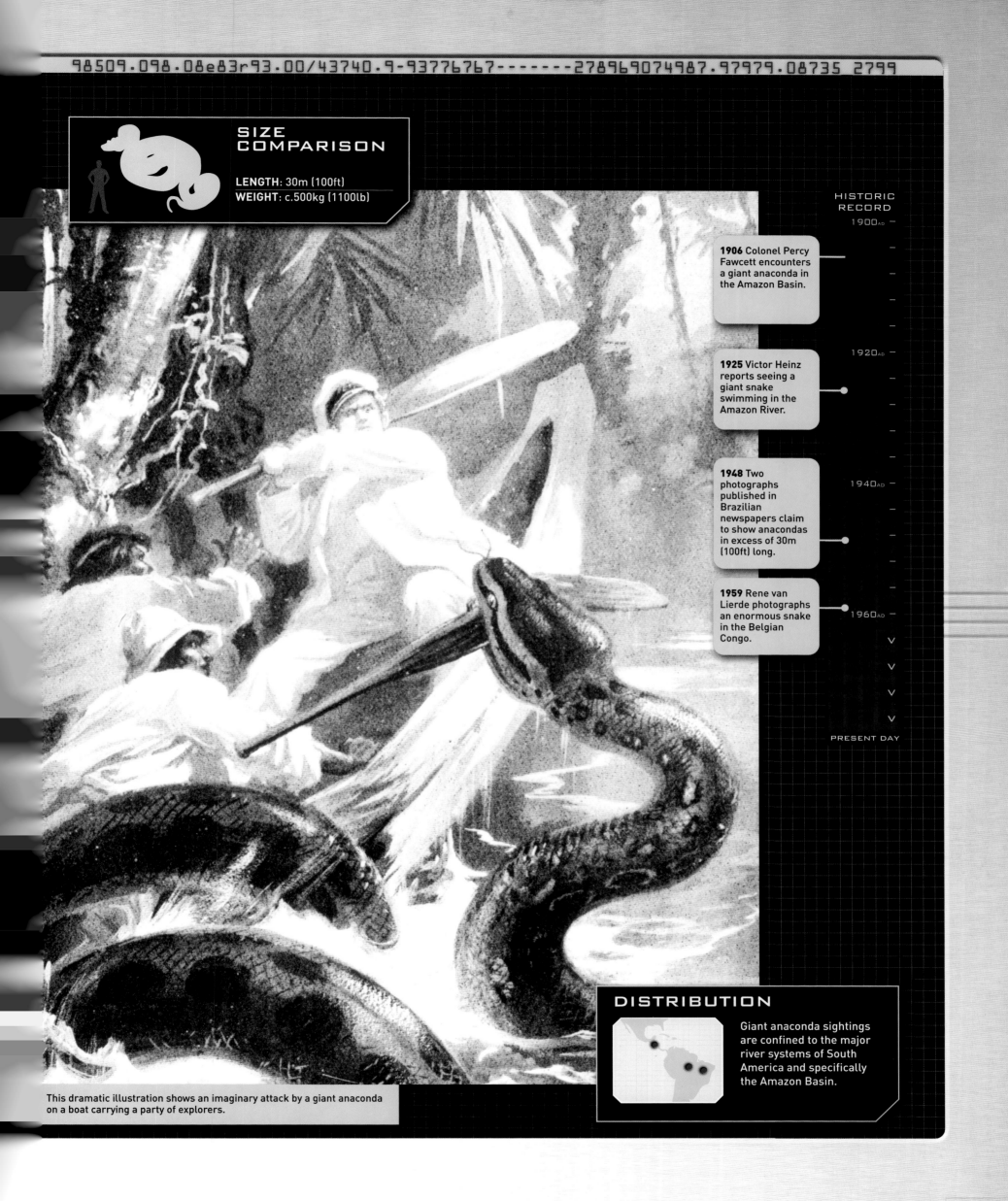

SIZE COMPARISON

LENGTH: 30m (100ft)
WEIGHT: c.500kg (1100lb)

HISTORIC RECORD

1900AD

1906 Colonel Percy Fawcett encounters a giant anaconda in the Amazon Basin.

1920AD

1925 Victor Heinz reports seeing a giant snake swimming in the Amazon River.

1940AD

1948 Two photographs published in Brazilian newspapers claim to show anacondas in excess of 30m (100ft) long.

1959 Rene van Lierde photographs an enormous snake in the Belgian Congo.

1960AD

PRESENT DAY

This dramatic illustration shows an imaginary attack by a giant anaconda on a boat carrying a party of explorers.

DISTRIBUTION

Giant anaconda sightings are confined to the major river systems of South America and specifically the Amazon Basin.

856/598509.098.08e83r93.00/43740.9-93776767------2786940?
8.00/43740.9-93776767------2789690749987.97979.08735

THE FEATHERED SERPENT

For centuries before the arrival of European settlers, many of the Mesoamerican peoples of central America worshipped a god in the form of a feathered serpent. Best known by the Aztec name Quetzalcoatl, this god was associated with winds, the dawn and the planet Venus. But could such a creature be a distorted recollection of a real animal – a flying lizard or feathered snake from the jungles of South America?

EVIDENCE

AN AMERICAN PTEROSAUR?
Some believe that feathered serpent legends were inspired by pterosaur reptiles surviving in the South American jungle. But Mesoamerican art is full of snake imagery (right), and there is nothing that resembles a pterosaur. In the early 1900s, several swarms of flying snakes were seen in the United States.

REAL FLYING SNAKES
Some known snakes have an ability that comes close to flying. Southeast Asian tree snakes launch themselves off high branches and flatten their ribcages to aid gliding. Perhaps an unknown South American snake shares this ability?

999790790.789.7

DISTRIBUTION

Legends of the feathered serpent god are found in Mesoamerican cultures stretching from Mexico down into South America.

HABITAT The feathered serpent is associated with the sky and winds, suggesting that any creature giving rise to the myth was largely airborne.

DIET Quetzalcoatl was typically worshipped with animal sacrifices, but apparently rejected human ones – an indication of the feeding habits of a real creature?

TRACKS AND SIGNS

Sculptures of Quetzalcoatl are found across the Mesoamerican world, often depicting the god in the form of a human with a feathered headdress, or as a half-human, half-serpent hybrid.

POTENTIAL RISK: LOW

The tradition of Quetzalcoatl rejecting human sacrifices may suggest that any real animal at the root of the legend is not a direct threat to humans.

SIZE COMPARISON

LENGTH: 6m (20ft)
WEIGHT: 130kg (290lb)

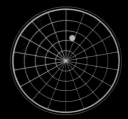

PROXIMITY STATUS

SUBJECT HIGHLY MOBILE AND AGGRESSIVE – MAINTAIN SAFE DISTANCE

163904567598509.098.08e83r93.00/43740.9-93776767------2789690749987.97979.08735

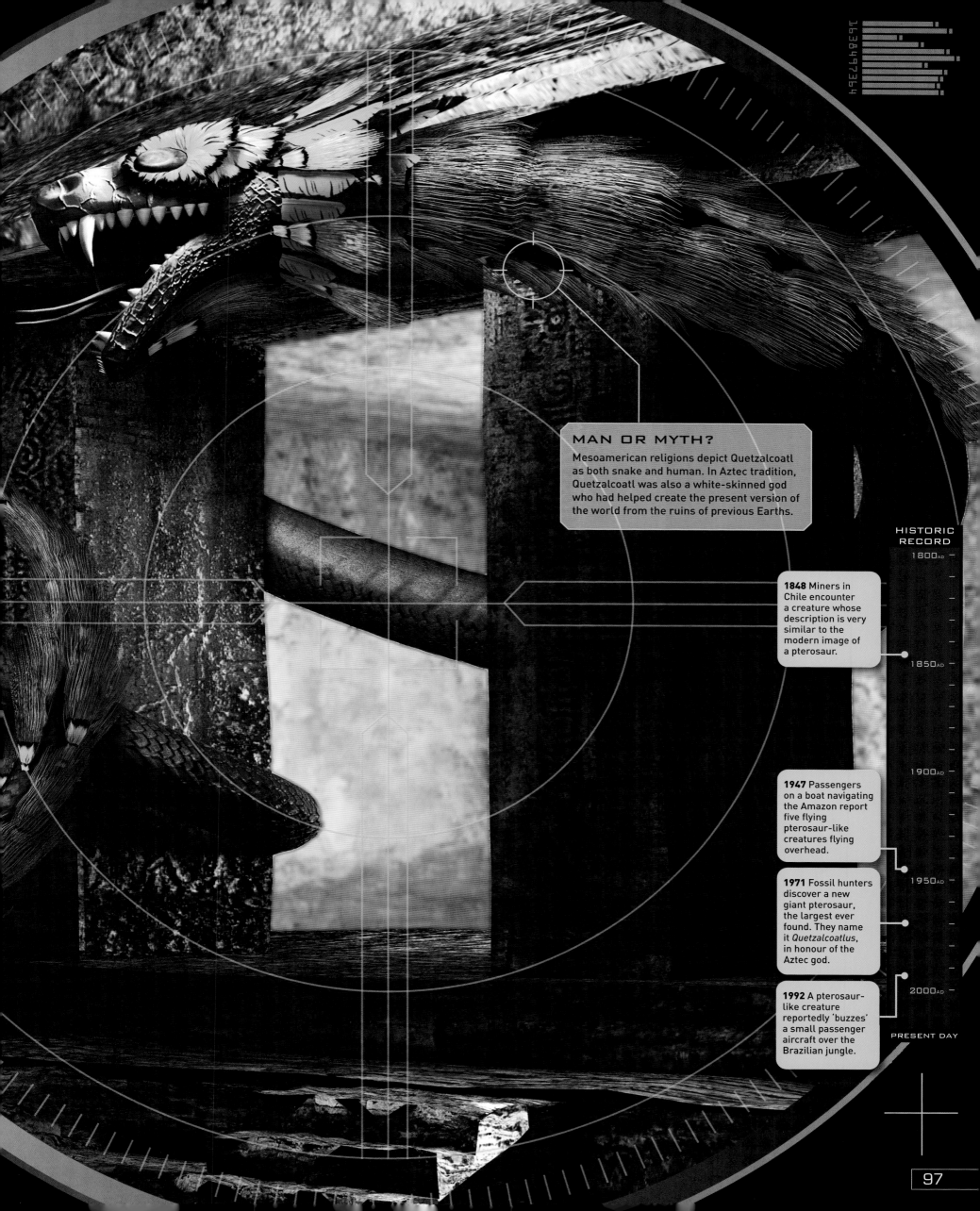

MAN OR MYTH?

Mesoamerican religions depict Quetzalcoatl as both snake and human. In Aztec tradition, Quetzalcoatl was also a white-skinned god who had helped create the present version of the world from the ruins of previous Earths.

1800ᴀᴅ —

1848 Miners in Chile encounter a creature whose description is very similar to the modern image of a pterosaur.

1850ᴀᴅ —

1900ᴀᴅ —

1947 Passengers on a boat navigating the Amazon report five flying pterosaur-like creatures flying overhead.

1950ᴀᴅ —

1971 Fossil hunters discover a new giant pterosaur, the largest ever found. They name it *Quetzalcoatlus*, in honour of the Aztec god.

2000ᴀᴅ —

1992 A pterosaur-like creature reportedly 'buzzes' a small passenger aircraft over the Brazilian jungle.

PRESENT DAY

163904567598509.098.08e83r93.00/43740.9-93776767------27896907

e83r93.00/43740.9-93776767------278969074987.97979.08735

MONSTERS OF SEA AND AIR

Some creatures refuse to be confined by geography – instead they roam freely around the world, following ocean currents or winds in the atmosphere. They include some of the earliest recorded monsters – sea serpents and mermaids – as well as bizarre creatures that are said to inhabit our atmosphere and which have only been discovered in modern times. Perhaps the most terrifying, however, are two marine giants – the colossal kraken and megalodon, the biggest shark that ever lived.

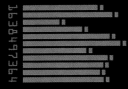

16390456759850‧09⁸‧08e83r93‧00/43740‧9-93776767------278969074987‧97979

SEA SERPENTS

A sailor's story or a real monster of the oceans? Sea serpents have been spotted emerging from the waves for centuries, with the first such creatures found in folklore from across the ancient world. More recently, some claim to have had much closer encounters. But reports often contradict each other and the appearance of the creatures varies from one sighting to the next. If sea serpents are real, what are they?

Swedish cleric Olaus Magnus wrote about a classic sea serpent in his 1555 history of the oceans. This monster, called the 'Sea Orm', was said to live in a submerged cave near the Norwegian city of Bergen. It emerged to snatch unwary livestock from fields along the shore, and occasionally attacked unfortunate vessels, plucking sailors from their decks.

Yet the Sea Orm is just one of countless sea serpents encountered through the centuries. Off Europe, they seem to be more common in far northern waters around Scandinavia and near Iceland. In North America, the coast of New England seems to be a particularly rich hunting ground. And every seagoing nation has its own tales to tell.

Sea serpents are one of the most frustrating creatures for cryptozoologists because they appear to come in a wide variety of forms. And although there are hundreds of reported sightings (including lengthy encounters with animals seen by dozens of people), most happened before the invention of the camera.

One convincing report, for example, came in 1848 from the captain and crew of HMS *Daedelus*. At sea in the South Atlantic, they encountered a monster roughly 18m (60ft) long, which swam with its head above water and according to one witness had a lizard-like appearance. The beast approached close to the ship and remained in sight for some 20 minutes, allowing those on board to make detailed sketches.

Bernard Heuvelmans, the father of cryptozoology, invented a classification system for sea serpents that included groups such as 'super-eel', 'many-humped' and 'mer-horse'. One of the most popular ideas is that sea serpents are in fact surviving plesiosaurs – a group of long-necked marine reptiles that lived in the time of the dinosaurs. But it's more likely that any real serpents are

in fact bizarre fish or undiscovered sea-going mammals.

Occasional decayed remains washed up on the coast only confuse matters further. When an animal dies at sea, the decay can do strange things to its appearance. The skin of whales, for example, can break up into fibrous 'fur'. In 1977, a Japanese trawler pulled up something that looked strikingly like a plesiosaur carcass – it later proved to be the remains of a basking shark.

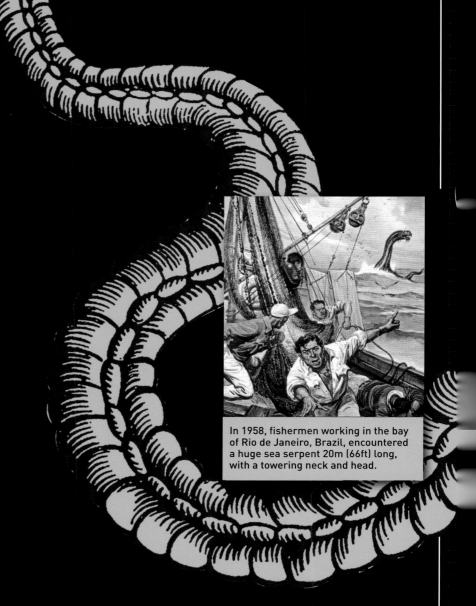

In 1958, fishermen working in the bay of Rio de Janeiro, Brazil, encountered a huge sea serpent 20m (66ft) long, with a towering neck and head.

98509.098.08e83r93.00/43740.9-9377676?------278969074987.97979.08735 2799

EVIDENCE

THE TRUTH BEHIND THE MYTH?
There's one spectacular and little-known sea creature that could explain at least some reports of sea serpents. Oarfish such as the 'king of herrings', *Regalecus glesne* (below), can grow up to 11m (36ft) long, have a comb-like fin on their heads and are thought to spend much of their time hanging vertically in the water. If they emerged, they could look very like the classic 'long-necked' sea serpent. Other possible explanations for different serpent types include misidentified whales and even the tentacles of giant squid.

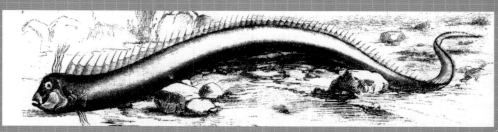

DISTRIBUTION

Sea serpent reports and legends come from all around the world, with particular hotspots in Arctic Ocean and the US eastern seaboard.

HISTORIC RECORD

1500AD

1555 Olaus Magnus describes the Sea Orm of Bergen.

1600AD

1638 First reports of a sea serpent off the coast of New England.

1700AD

1734 Hans Egede, Bishop of Greenland, has a close encounter with a sea serpent whose head towers taller than the mainmast of his ship.

1845 German naturalist Hans Koch attempts to reconstruct a sea serpent he calls *Hydrarchos*, based on various bones from fossil whales.

1800AD

1848 HMS *Daedelus* has a lengthy encounter with a sea serpent.

1900AD

1937 A supposed sea serpent carcass is retrieved from the stomach of a sperm whale off the coast of Canada.

2000AD

PRESENT DAY

SIZE COMPARISON

LENGTH: c. 30m (100ft)
WEIGHT: c.25,000kg (55,000lb)

DISTRIBUTION

Kraken legends come mostly from Arctic seas, but they are probably found in cold ocean depths worldwide.

THE KRAKEN

Scandinavian seafarers tell stories of monstrous tentacled creatures that slumber on the seabeds around Norway and Iceland. These krakens are usually thought to be an undiscovered species of colossal octopus. They emerge at the surface only rarely and are so large that they can be mistaken for new islands, creating towering waves that ripple out across vast areas of sea. Their powerful tentacles can pull down the largest ships, and the whirlpools created when they submerge again can drag any survivors to their doom. They are truly the stuff of sailors' nightmares.

300

250

200

AUTO   150

100

50

0

EVIDENCE

EARLY TALES

Krakens were known by other names in old Norse sagas, but there are clear references to these creatures from around the 1200s. In the 18th century, Swedish naturalist Carolus Linnaeus included the kraken in his first great catalogue of life, the *Systema Naturae*.

SHIP KILLER?

In 1802, French scientist Pierre Denys de Montfort blamed the kraken for the loss of several sailing ships (right). Today, many biologists believe that kraken legends were inspired by sightings of the giant squid, but some reports described creatures far larger than any currently known squid.

PROXIMITY STATUS

WARNING: SUBJECT SURFACING – BRACE FOR BACKWASH!

HABITAT These enormous monsters are said to spend most of their time in a dormant state on the seabed, rising to the surface only rarely.

DIET Krakens are said to lie at the heart of their own ecosystem, feeding on small numbers of fish while their waste nourishes huge shoals around them.

TRACKS AND SIGNS

Scandinavian fishermen believe that the locations of slumbering krakens are marked by rich fishing grounds. These enormous beasts may also be responsible for mysterious low-frequency noises sometimes detected underwater.

FLOATING ISLAND?

Early descriptions of the kraken give this animal huge dimensions – perhaps several kilometres across. Some have suggested that these stories of temporary islands and dangerous whirlpools could be inspired by undersea volcanoes around Iceland.

HISTORIC RECORD

1000 AD

c.1250 Norwegian sagas describe sea monsters later identified as krakens.

1500 AD

1752 Erik Pontoppidan describes the kraken in detail in his *Natural History of Norway*.

1802 Pierre Denys de Montfort blames the kraken for the loss of a whaling ship off Angola.

2000 AD

PRESENT DAY

1857 The giant squid is first recognized by science, providing a convenient explanation for later kraken sightings.

SIZE COMPARISON

LENGTH: 30–600m (100–2000ft)
WEIGHT: Unknown

POTENTIAL RISK: HIGH

The sheer size of the kraken makes it a great danger to any seagoing vessel, although there is less evidence for direct attacks on shipping.

MEGALODON

Just a few million years ago, the oceans were ruled by a truly monstrous creature – a giant shark that may have grown to almost the size of a modern blue whale. Closely related to the fearsome great white shark, *Carcharodon megalodon* was several times the size and would have been a vicious predator, with teeth some 18cm (7in) long. But is this nightmare shark as dead as scientists believe? Officially extinct for around 1.5 million years, some intriguing fossils suggest that the beast might have survived into historical times. Blood-chilling tales of encounters with gargantuan sharks add to the evidence.

300 —

250 —

200 —

AUTO 150 —

➤

100 —

50 —

0 —

TRACKS AND SIGNS

Sightings of megalodon-type sharks are rare, indicating that these monsters normally reside in the deepest oceans. This contradicts fossil evidence that megalodon originally hunted whales in shallow tropical waters.

☠☠☠☠☠
✖✖✖✖✖

POTENTIAL RISK: EXTREME

Megalodon was quite simply the largest predator the world has ever known. Any surviving specimens must be monstrous killing machines capable of attacking a medium-sized boat. Fortunately, if megalodon is still out there it has made an evolutionary retreat from surface waters.

PROXIMITY STATUS

SUBJECT DISTRACTED BUT DANGEROUS – REMAIN STATIONARY

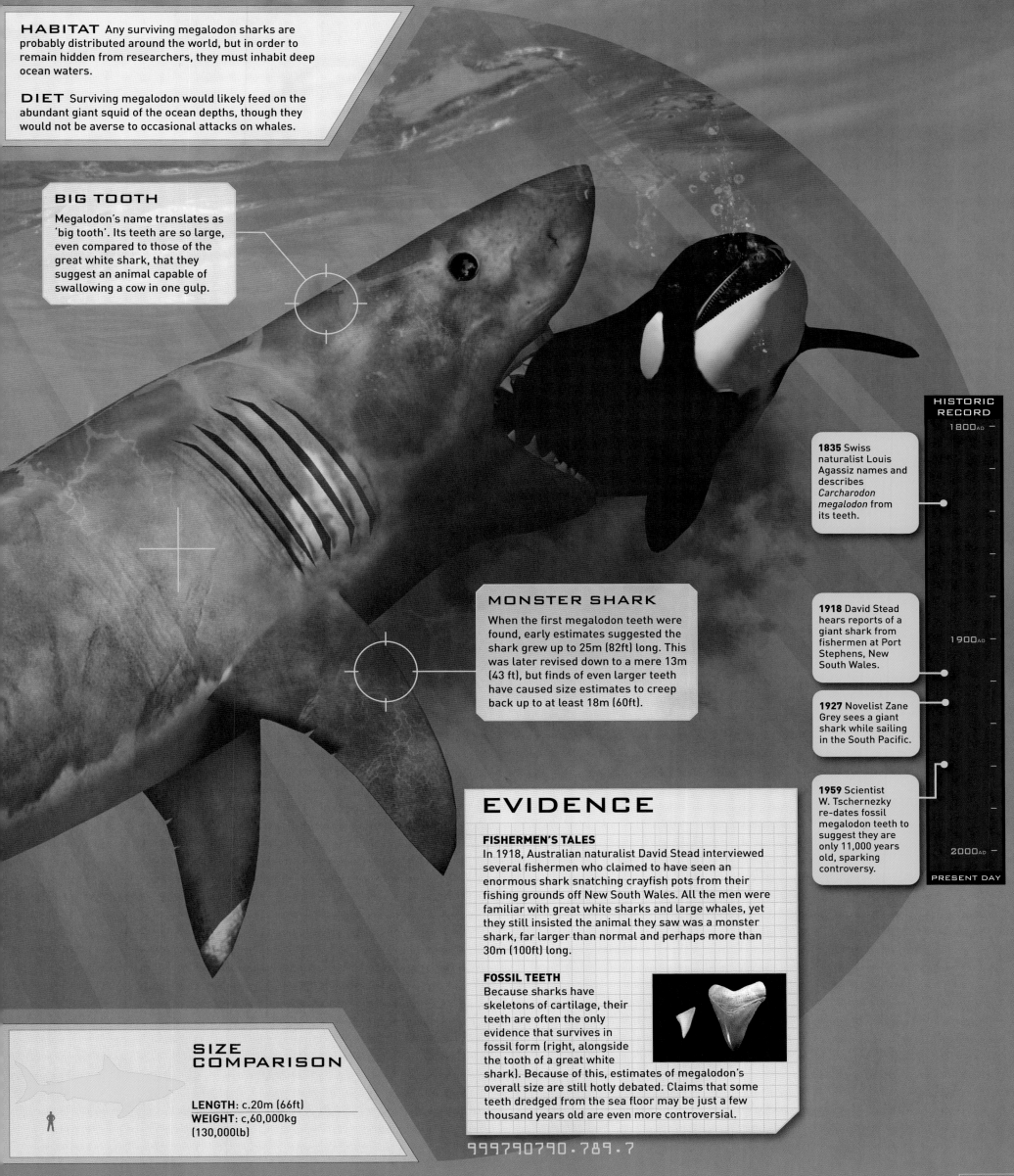

HABITAT Any surviving megalodon sharks are probably distributed around the world, but in order to remain hidden from researchers, they must inhabit deep ocean waters.

DIET Surviving megalodon would likely feed on the abundant giant squid of the ocean depths, though they would not be averse to occasional attacks on whales.

BIG TOOTH

Megalodon's name translates as 'big tooth'. Its teeth are so large, even compared to those of the great white shark, that they suggest an animal capable of swallowing a cow in one gulp.

MONSTER SHARK

When the first megalodon teeth were found, early estimates suggested the shark grew up to 25m (82ft) long. This was later revised down to a mere 13m (43 ft), but finds of even larger teeth have caused size estimates to creep back up to at least 18m (60ft).

EVIDENCE

FISHERMEN'S TALES
In 1918, Australian naturalist David Stead interviewed several fishermen who claimed to have seen an enormous shark snatching crayfish pots from their fishing grounds off New South Wales. All the men were familiar with great white sharks and large whales, yet they still insisted the animal they saw was a monster shark, far larger than normal and perhaps more than 30m (100ft) long.

FOSSIL TEETH
Because sharks have skeletons of cartilage, their teeth are often the only evidence that survives in fossil form (right, alongside the tooth of a great white shark). Because of this, estimates of megalodon's overall size are still hotly debated. Claims that some teeth dredged from the sea floor may be just a few thousand years old are even more controversial.

SIZE COMPARISON

LENGTH: c.20m (66ft)
WEIGHT: c,60,000kg (130,000lb)

HISTORIC RECORD

1800AD

1835 Swiss naturalist Louis Agassiz names and describes *Carcharodon megalodon* from its teeth.

1900AD

1918 David Stead hears reports of a giant shark from fishermen at Port Stephens, New South Wales.

1927 Novelist Zane Grey sees a giant shark while sailing in the South Pacific.

1959 Scientist W. Tschernezky re-dates fossil megalodon teeth to suggest they are only 11,000 years old, sparking controversy.

2000AD

PRESENT DAY

16390456759850 9.098.08e83r93.00/43740.9-9377676 7------278969074987.97979

MERMAIDS AND MERMEN

Ever since people first went to sea, they have encountered creatures with the upper body of a woman or man, and the lower half of a fish. Powerful swimmers, mermaids and mermen are sometimes seen on the shore and sometimes swimming alongside boats. Often they are depicted as friendly creatures, saving drowning people, helping ships in distress, and sometimes even falling in love with humans, but other mer-people have a dark side, luring vessels to their doom and even drowning sailors deliberately.

The first mermaid was the ancient Syrian goddess Atargatis, who was said to have begun life as a beautiful woman who fell in love with a mortal man and, when she fell pregnant, threw herself into the sea in shame, hoping to hide herself in the form of a fish. The waters, however, refused to conceal her beauty, so she found herself still human from the waist up. In reverence for their goddess, the Syrians refused to eat fish. Tales of Atargatis spread around the ancient world, and soon the mermaid was known under various names – in Greece, for example, she was called Derketo.

In later times, mer-people developed into an entire hidden civilization, complete with underwater cities and a complex culture. In some Greek tales, mermaids are presented as sirens (see p.30), luring men with their beautiful song, and either causing their deaths, or taking them away to undersea worlds, never to be seen again.

The stories of the *Arabian Nights* reveal even more about the undersea world. In one tale, Abdullah the Fishermen visits an undersea world where the society is a mirror-image of his own life on the land. Other stories reveal that this waterworld was once an advanced civilization on dry land, before being submerged beneath the waves – rather like the Greek tales of Atlantis.

In northwest Europe, mermaids are seen as simpler creatures, related to the fairies. Some are sirens and ship-wreckers, and others, if not actually wicked, are still omens of coming danger. Most, however, are fairly friendly on those rare occasions when they come into contact with people – though they do not necessarily understand human ways. The Irish merman Coomara, for instance, trapped the souls of drowned fishermen in cages, not understanding that they would rather go free.

The people of Zennor in Cornwall, meanwhile, still tell of a mermaid called Morveren, who fell in love with the village youth Mathew Trewela after hearing his beautiful singing. Desperate to see him, she struggled ashore with a dress to disguise her tail, only to be discovered. Fortunately, the story had a happy ending – the young man fell in love with her at first sight, and while she could never live on land, he could go with her to live beneath the sea. To this day, they say you can still hear his singing from beneath the waves, and that the tone of his song warns the village fishermen of coming storms. Hans Christian Andersen's 1837 story of *The Little Mermaid* tells the reverse tale of a mermaid willing to give up her life in the sea for the love of a human prince.

EVIDENCE

FEEJEE MERMAIDS AND JENNY HANNIVERS
For centuries, hoaxers have exploited peoples' fascination for mermaids by making ingenious fakes. The famous US circus owner P.T. Barnum made a small fortune by displaying his 'Feejee mermaid' for more than 20 years. In reality, this creature was a fake made by joining the upper half of a monkey skeleton to the tail of a fish – although the original was lost in a fire, it inspired several copies (right). Long before Barnum's time, Belgian fishermen amused themselves by carving the dried bodies of skates and other fish into grotesque mer-people known as Jenny Hannivers.

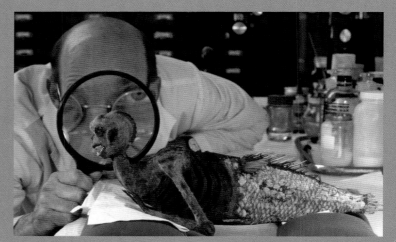

98509.098.08e83r93.00/43740.9-93776767------278969074987.97979.08735 2799

SIZE COMPARISON

LENGTH: 1.8m (6ft)
WEIGHT: 70kg (155lb)

DISTRIBUTION

Mermaid stories and sightings have a global distribution, but the strongest traditions are found on Europe's Atlantic coast.

Although mermaid sightings have declined since the 19th century, they still happen occasionally. Italian fisherman Colmaro Orsino had a close encounter with this mermaid at Bocca di Magra in 1962.

HISTORIC RECORD

1000AD —

1167 Fishermen in the village of Orford, Suffolk, in eastern England, capture a merman who later escapes.

1608 Explorer Henry Hudson and his crew see a mermaid while at sea near Norway.

1500AD —

1614 American colonist John Smith reports a close encounter with a mermaid.

1842 P.T. Barnum announces his display of the fabulous 'Feejee Mermaid'.

1890 A wave of mermaid sightings around Orkney reach their peak.

2000AD —

PRESENT DAY

During the 18th century, some artists depicted mer-people as an underwater civilization, complete with their own animals such as mer-horses and even mer-dogs!

DISTRIBUTION

Strange atmospheric phenomena, more organic than traditional UFOs, have been seen all around the world.

BEASTS OF THE ATMOSPHERE

Strange reports of organic material falling from the sky – blood-like 'red rain' or unidentified jelly-like materials – point to a startling possibility. Could there be huge, ethereal animals floating in the upper levels of Earth's atmosphere? These bizarre creatures could also explain a variety of peculiar UFO sightings and other mysterious objects sometimes seen in the sky. Since the late 1950s, researchers have claimed to photograph these organisms, often using heat-sensitive infrared cameras, but the jury is still out on this.

EVIDENCE

THE CRAWFORDSVILLE MONSTER

In September 1891, the residents of Crawfordsville, Indiana, were startled by a strange apparition in the night sky – a one-eyed aerial creature that propelled itself through the air with multiple sets of fins. The creature returned the following night and appeared to be in distress. After that, it was never seen again.

LIFE IN JUPITER?

In the early 1960s respected NASA scientist Carl Sagan suggested that aerial creatures could have evolved in the deep atmospheres of gas giant planets such as Jupiter. Such creatures might resemble ocean animals like jellyfish and rays, which are strangely similar to some 'sky critters' seen by eyewitnesses on Earth.

TRACKS AND SIGNS

Aerial organisms seem to be largely invisible – perhaps they only become opaque in certain atmospheric conditions. Infrared cameras and even normal video cameras seem to be more sensitive to these strange beasts.

PROXIMITY STATUS

HUGE BUT EXTREMELY FAINT ATMOSPHERIC DISRUPTION DETECTED

HABITAT These creatures seem to live at high altitudes, rarely descending to ground level.

DIET Atmospheric organisms may prey on each other or on more substantial creatures such as birds. Some researchers believe they extend tendrils to feed on energy from power lines.

01001110 1

_10011101

010000

FLOATING GASBAGS?

In order to stay aloft, any aerial organism has to be lighter than air. One possibility is that these creatures heat trapped air like a hot air balloon, or somehow produce a buoyant gas such as hydrogen or helium.

HISTORIC RECORD

1880AD —

1891 The 'Crawfordsville Monster' is seen in Indiana on two successive nights.

1900AD —

1931 US anomaly researcher Charles Fort suggests the existence of lighter-than-air animals in his book *Lo!*

1920AD —

1933 Frank Smythe, a mountaineer on an expedition attempting to climb Everest, encounters two strange balloon-like creatures at high altitude.

1947 During the first great wave of UFO sightings, US researcher John Philip Bessor suggests that the sightings might be some form of space animal.

1940AD —

1957 Trevor James Constable makes infrared photographs of 'amoeboid bioforms' above California's Mojave Desert.

1960AD —

∨
∨
∨
∨

PRESENT DAY

SIZE COMPARISON

LENGTH: c.500m (1650ft)
WEIGHT: Unknown

POTENTIAL RISK: LOW

By all accounts these enormous creatures are uninterested in the terrestrial world and do no harm to humans or other land animals. However, some people have suggested that encounters with 'sky critters' may be responsible for some otherwise inexplicable aviation mysteries.

1639045675985 09.098.08e83r93.00/43740.9-93776767------27896907
e83r93.00/43740.9-93776767------278969074987.97979.08735

AFRICAN BEASTS

The enormous continent of Africa still hides vast regions that have not been fully explored, and new species are discovered here regularly. But in some remote regions natives and explorers alike have reported encounters with truly amazing creatures – giant dinosaur-like reptiles, sharp-beaked flying lizards, and horrific predators. Are these monsters truly the prehistoric survivors they appear to be?

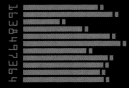

1639045675985 09.098.08e83r93.00/43740.9-93776767------

| | | | | | | | | | | | | | |

DISTRIBUTION

At the start of the 20th century, the Nandi bear was known from across Kenya. Today, however, its range is limited to the north of the country.

THE NANDI BEAR

Among the Nandi people of northern Kenya, tales are still told of a ferocious killer that roams at night and eats only the brains of its victims. This beast has many names, but is most widely known as the 'Nandi bear' on account of the way it was first described to western explorers. But today there are no known bears on the African continent, and cryptozoologists have long argued about the true identity of this mysterious predator. Could it be a descendant of the Atlas bears that once roamed north Africa, a giant baboon or a survivor from a once-common species of giant hyena?

POTENTIAL RISK: HIGH

Although Nandi killings are normally restricted to livestock, there are many native tales of the creatures entering villages at night and even breaking into huts to attack people. This seems to contradict the tales of colonial settlers, in which the animal seems to turn tail and run when confronted.

TRACKS AND SIGNS

The Nandi bear is a silent and secretive hunter, only venturing close to settlements on dark nights. It leaves large five-toed footprints that are easily distinguished from those of other large predators such as lions.

300

250

200

AUTO 150

100

50

0

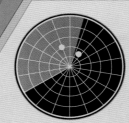

PROXIMITY STATUS

SUBJECT HAS NOTICED REMOTE CAMERA – REMAIN QUIET IN HIDE

16390456759850q·098·08e83r93·00/43740·9-93776767------278969074987·97979·08735

HABITAT This mysterious predator spends most of its time in forests, only emerging into the open at night.

DIET The Nandi bear is said to prey mostly on livestock, though it will also attack people when given the opportunity. Its habit of eating the brains of its victims has been seen in some spotted hyenas – further evidence that it may be related to them.

EVIDENCE

COLONIAL TALES
Several white settlers in Kenya wrote of their close encounters with the Nandi bear in the early 20th century. Geoffrey Williams described it as 'larger than a bear... and quite as heavily built. The forequarters were thickly furred... and the head long and pointed and exactly like that of a bear.'

HYENA OR BABOON?
Perhaps the most convincing explanation for the Nandi bear is that it is a surviving form of the short-faced hyena, a lion-sized carnivore that roamed Africa until about 100,000 years ago. Other suggestions include a giant baboon (above) or a survivor of the Atlas bears that once roamed Africa.

999790790.789.7

SHORT-FACED KILLER

If the Nandi bear is a surviving short-faced hyena, then it is a daunting lion-sized killer with crushing jaws and aggressive temperament. However, some think that its 'brain-eating' killings might actually be the work of other animals.

HISTORIC RECORD

1900AD

1912 Geoffrey Williams' report brings the Nandi bear to the attention of the outside world.

1919 Farmer Cara Buxton finds a number of dead sheep with their brains torn out – killings that are attributed to a large hyena.

1920AD

1925 A Nandi village appeals for government help after a large wild animal abducts a small girl from a hut.

1940AD

1935 Palaeontologist Louis Leakey suggests that the Nandi bear may be a surviving prehistoric mammal called a *Chalicotherium*.

1960AD

1957 Estate manager Douglas Hutton shoots two animals whose skeletons are identified as 'giant forest hyenas' by the Nairobi Museum.

PRESENT DAY

SIZE COMPARISON

HEIGHT: 1.8m (6ft)
WEIGHT: 300kg (660lb)

6360387-080-0.32786465849409------999790790.789.7---87894689468940.0.0

DISTRIBUTION

The Ennedi tiger is known by various names across Chad and the northern Central African Republic.

THE ENNEDI TIGER

High on the Ennedi Plateau of northern Chad, and across the neighbouring Central African Republic, local people warn visitors of a fearsome predator that's larger and more powerful than a lion, and armed with a vicious pair of long, walrus-like teeth. Western hunters have also heard its cry, and native descriptions are remarkably consistent. Could this creature, known locally as the *tigre de montagne* or mountain tiger, be a living relic of the sabre-toothed cats that roamed across the world before the last ice age?

300

250

200

AUTO 150

100

50

0

☠ ☠ ☠ ☠ ☠

POTENTIAL RISK: MEDIUM

The Ennedi tiger is a fearless predator, but seems to avoid direct confrontation with humans. Although there are no known stories of attacks on people, this cat is more than capable of defending itself when cornered and so is best approached with caution.

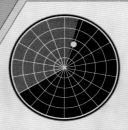

PROXIMITY STATUS

SUBJECTS CLOSE BUT DISTRACTED – REMAIN STILL AND DO NOT PROVOKE

HABITAT This 'tiger' avoids habitations and farmland, preferring to make its home among the caves of arid and mountainous wilderness areas.

DIET In general, the Ennedi tiger is thought to prey on wild antelopes, but it will tackle animals as large and ferocious as hippos when it has to.

TRACKS AND SIGNS

Kills made by this powerful hunter can be identified by the deep puncture wounds from its outsized canine teeth. However, the *tigre de montagne*'s habit of dragging its kills to the safety of a cave lair mean they are rarely found.

HISTORIC RECORD

1910 A French army officer sees a soldier attacked by a sabre-toothed 'water lion' as he leads a column across the Bamingui River in what is now the Central African Republic.

1937 Colonist Lucien Blancou learns from a tribal elder about a lion-sized red cat called the grassingram in the Central African Republiic.

c.1963 Christian le Noel first hears tales of the *tigre de montagne*.

1900AD
1920AD
1940AD
1960AD
1980AD

PRESENT DAY

TIGER STRIPES

One of the most convincing pieces of evidence for the Ennedi tiger's existence is the consistency of native descriptions. It is always described as sabre-toothed and short-tailed, with powerful forelimbs and a reddish coat with white stripes.

EVIDENCE

THE MOUNTAIN TIGER

During the 1960s, experienced French hunter Christian le Noel was investigating a mountain ravine in the Central African Republic, when he heard the roar of a big cat that he did not recognize. His guide warned him that this was the *tigre de montagne*, and refused to go any further despite the fact that they were well-armed.

ANOTHER SABRE-TOOTHED CAT?

Surprisingly, the people of this area describe not just one sabre-toothed cat, but a second species that has a long tail and lives mostly in the water. This 'water lion' is said to eat mostly fish, but will also attack other animals.

SIZE COMPARISON

HEIGHT: 1.5m (5ft)
WEIGHT: 240kg (530lb)

KONGAMATO

The Kaonde people of Zambia live in fear of a terrible bird that flies slowly and silently over the Jiundu swamps, overturning boats and attacking fishermen. But this bird has no feathers – instead its wings are covered in a leathery membrane and its beak is a terrible sharpened weapon. In fact, this creature, known locally as *Kongamato* ('the breaker of boats'), sounds more like a prehistoric pterosaur than a modern bird. Is it possible that flying reptiles, thought to have gone extinct alongside the dinosaurs some 65 million years ago, still survive in the depths of the African swamp?

EVIDENCE

IN WITCHBOUND AFRICA

In 1923, British administrator Frank H. Melland wrote *In Witchbound Africa*, an account of his time among the peoples of northern Rhodesia (modern Zambia). He was the first to hear native tales of *Kongamato*. Intrigued, he conducted a test, showing an eyewitness pictures of a variety of living and extinct flying animals. The terrified man insisted that a pterosaur was the closest match to *Kongamato*.

WINGED GIANTS

Sightings of *Kongamato* suggest that it is a relatively small pterosaur, with a wingspan of up to 2m (6.7ft). But other areas of Africa, such as the Namib Desert, have produced reports of much larger flying reptiles.

999790790.789.7

DISTRIBUTION

Pterosaur-like creatures are reported from across much of central and southern Africa.

HABITAT These creatures are usually found in remote swamp areas with few human inhabitants.

DIET Pterosaurs matching the description of *Kongamato* are believed to have been fish-eaters, perhaps explaining their attacks on fishermen.

TRACKS AND SIGNS

Kongamato is a silent glider that attacks without warning. It is said to get its name from its trick of diving into the water and surfacing beneath fishing boats, tipping out their defenceless occupants.

POTENTIAL RISK: HIGH

This flying reptile is too small to treat people as prey, but its sharp beak is still capable of inflicting severe wounds.

SIZE COMPARISON

LENGTH: 1m (3.3ft)
WINGSPAN: 2m (6.7ft)
WEIGHT: 4kg 9lb)

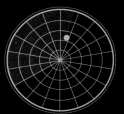

PROXIMITY STATUS

SUBJECT IN FLIGHT – MAINTAIN SAFE DISTANCE AND CONTINUE OBSERVATIONS

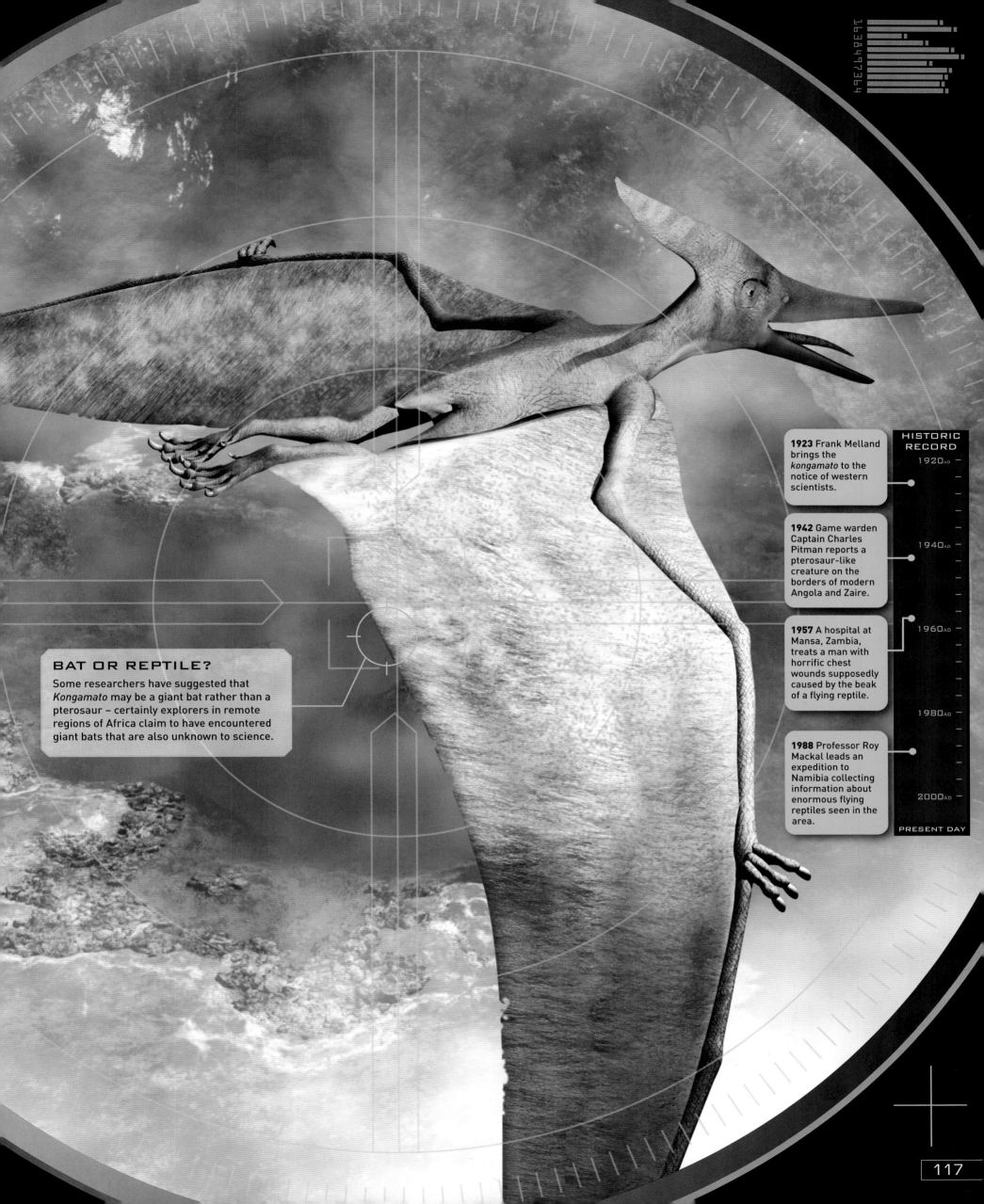

BAT OR REPTILE?

Some researchers have suggested that *Kongamato* may be a giant bat rather than a pterosaur – certainly explorers in remote regions of Africa claim to have encountered giant bats that are also unknown to science.

1923 Frank Melland brings the *kongamato* to the notice of western scientists.

1920ᴬᴰ

1942 Game warden Captain Charles Pitman reports a pterosaur-like creature on the borders of modern Angola and Zaire.

1940ᴬᴰ

1957 A hospital at Mansa, Zambia, treats a man with horrific chest wounds supposedly caused by the beak of a flying reptile.

1960ᴬᴰ

1980ᴬᴰ

1988 Professor Roy Mackal leads an expedition to Namibia collecting information about enormous flying reptiles seen in the area.

2000ᴬᴰ

PRESENT DAY

DISTRIBUTION

The majority of recent reports have focussed on the Lake Tele region of the Congo, but earlier sightings suggest a range extending to Zambia.

MOKELE MBEMBE

For more than a century, explorers in the African jungles of the Congo River Basin have heard reports of a monstrous, long-necked creature known in the local Lingala language as *Mokele Mbembe* – 'the one who stops the flow of rivers'. Many accounts suggest the creature is reptilian, and native descriptions match remarkably well with the long-necked plant-eating dinosaurs known as sauropods. These creatures include well-known animals such as *Diplodocus* and *Apatosaurus*, and are thought to have been extinct for at least 65 million years. Could a living dinosaur really survive today in the African swamps?

300 —

250 —

200 —

AUTO 150 —

100 —

50 —

0 —

LONG-NECKED HERBIVORE

Long necks are thought to have evolved so that sauropod dinosaurs could reach inaccessible vegetation. Despite the enormous size of their bodies, these animals have tiny brains and limited intelligence.

TRACKS AND SIGNS

The enormous size and weight of these creatures means that, in the right conditions, they leave large, deep foot-prints on the forest floor. Explorers have also reported eerie and unique calls – perhaps for communication with the herd.

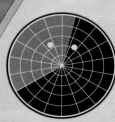

PROXIMITY STATUS

SUBJECTS APPPEAR CALM – MAINTAIN DISTANCE AND DO NOT DISTURB

16390467598509·098·08e83r93·00/43740·9·93776767------278969074987·97979·08735

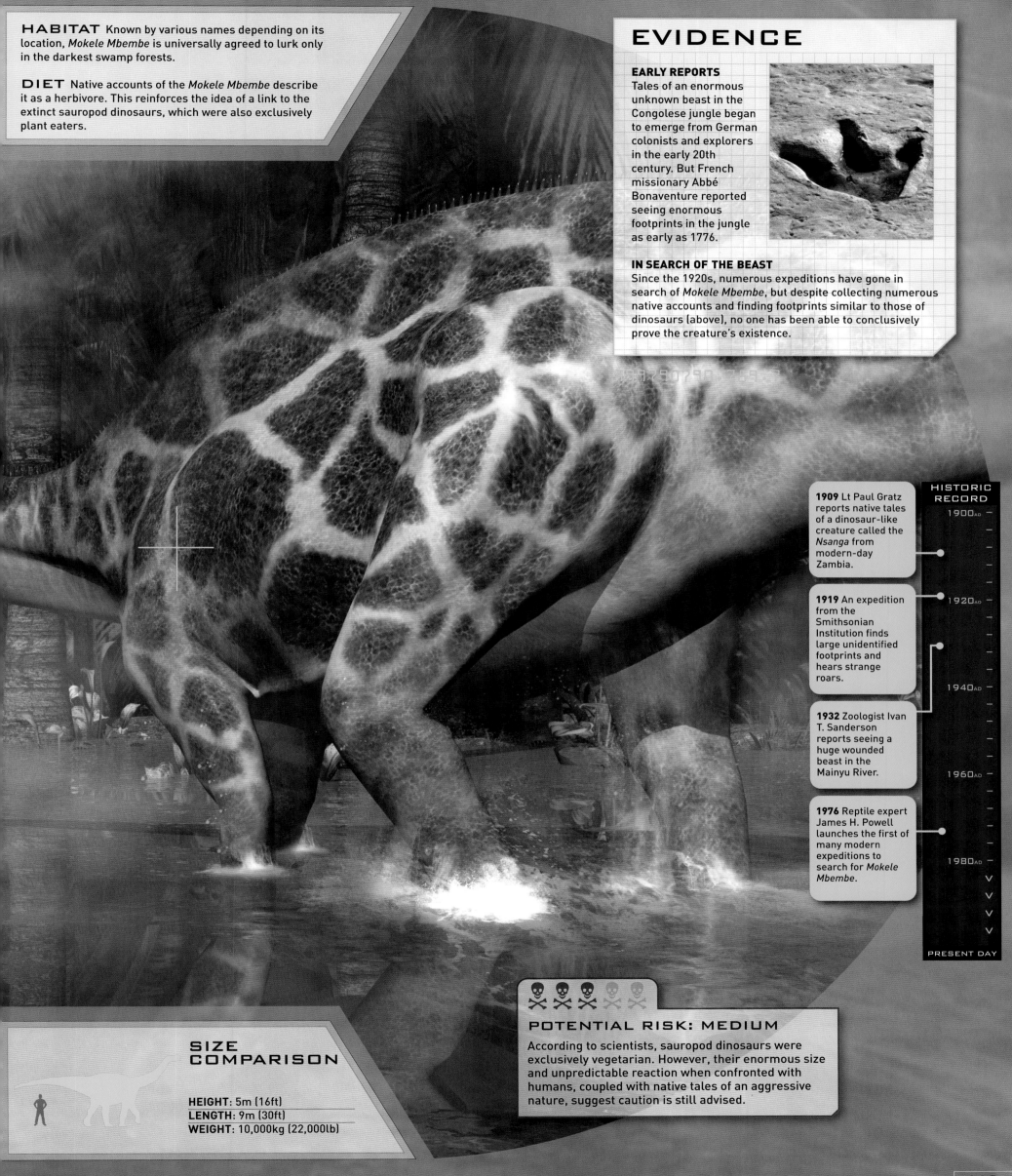

HABITAT Known by various names depending on its location, *Mokele Mbembe* is universally agreed to lurk only in the darkest swamp forests.

DIET Native accounts of the *Mokele Mbembe* describe it as a herbivore. This reinforces the idea of a link to the extinct sauropod dinosaurs, which were also exclusively plant eaters.

EVIDENCE

EARLY REPORTS
Tales of an enormous unknown beast in the Congolese jungle began to emerge from German colonists and explorers in the early 20th century. But French missionary Abbé Bonaventure reported seeing enormous footprints in the jungle as early as 1776.

IN SEARCH OF THE BEAST
Since the 1920s, numerous expeditions have gone in search of *Mokele Mbembe*, but despite collecting numerous native accounts and finding footprints similar to those of dinosaurs (above), no one has been able to conclusively prove the creature's existence.

HISTORIC RECORD

1909 Lt Paul Gratz reports native tales of a dinosaur-like creature called the *Nsanga* from modern-day Zambia.

1919 An expedition from the Smithsonian Institution finds large unidentified footprints and hears strange roars.

1932 Zoologist Ivan T. Sanderson reports seeing a huge wounded beast in the Mainyu River.

1976 Reptile expert James H. Powell launches the first of many modern expeditions to search for *Mokele Mbembe*.

1900AD
1920AD
1940AD
1960AD
1980AD

PRESENT DAY

SIZE COMPARISON

HEIGHT: 5m (16ft)
LENGTH: 9m (30ft)
WEIGHT: 10,000kg (22,000lb)

POTENTIAL RISK: MEDIUM

According to scientists, sauropod dinosaurs were exclusively vegetarian. However, their enormous size and unpredictable reaction when confronted with humans, coupled with native tales of an aggressive nature, suggest caution is still advised.

16390456759850**09.098.08e83r93.00/43740.9-93776767------27896907**

e83r93.00/43740.9-93776767------278969074987.97979.08735

ASIA AND
BEYOND

The vast expanses of Asia, its countless bounding islands, and the isolated continent of Australia are filled with a rich variety of mysterious creatures. They range from legends apparently come to life, such as the Vietnamese *naga*, to animals that are widely thought to be extinct, including the enormous Australian lizard *Megalania*. These lands are also home to some of the most intriguing and human-like of creatures – the yeti of the Himalayan plateau, and the *orang pendek* of the Indonesian islands.

16390456759850**09.098.08e83r93.00/43740.9-93776767------**

DISTRIBUTION

Originating on the steppes of Central Asia, gryphons have spread widely across Eurasia, although sightings are rare.

THE GRYPHON

Among the most majestic of all fabulous beasts, the gryphon combines the body of a lion with the head and wings of an eagle. It is a ferocious but noble predator with a dragon-like tendency to hoard gold. Although they first appear in literature around the 5th century BC – when Greek writers associated them with central Asian regions beyond the Ural Mountains – gryphon legends go back much further than that. Amazingly, the mummified remains of warriors from the gryphon's homelands, preserved for perhaps 3,000 years, display tattoos of the animals on their skin.

MATING HABITS

Gryphons pair for life and when one partner dies, the other never seeks a new mate. However, there are rare tales of gryphons mating with horses to produce a rare hybrid animal – the hippogriff.

300 —

250 —

200 —

AUTO 150 —

100 —

50 —

0 —

PROXIMITY STATUS

WARNING: SUBJECTS DANGEROUS BUT DISTRACTED – MAINTAIN CAUTION

HABITAT These ferocious animals are found in remote wilderness and mountainous regions.

DIET Gryphons are partial to human flesh when provoked, but are famed for attacking horses. Their hatred of horses supposedly developed as a result of their ancient clashes with the cavalry of the Arimaspians and has today become instinctive.

☠☠☠☠☠
☠☠☠☠☠

POTENTIAL RISK: HIGH

Beautiful though gryphons undeniably are, they are also armed with a vicious beak, claws and talons. They are best approached with extreme caution – any signs of confrontation or aggression are likely to be met with an immediate attack.

010011
101_10
011101
010000

123

NOBLE BEAST

The gryphon's fusion of features from animals of land and air has made it a popular symbol throughout history. The Christian church, for example, saw it as a representation of the half-divine, half-mortal Jesus.

500BC

c.450BC Greek historian Herodotus writes an account of the war between the gryphons and the Arimaspians, based on a lost work by an earlier writer.

0AD

c.400BC Greek physician Ctesias reports Persian beliefs about gryphons.

c.70AD Pliny the Elder provides a detailed description of gryphons in his *Natural History*.

500AD

520 Irish explorer St Brendan's ship is attacked by a lone gryphon during a long sea voyage.

1000AD

PRESENT DAY

TRACKS AND SIGNS

Before mating, male and female gryphons frequently indulge in noisy courtship battles that draw attention to these otherwise elusive creatures.

EVIDENCE

GREEK REPORTS

According to the Greeks, gryphons lived in Central Asia, where they fought with cyclops-like people called the Arimaspians over the gold from the rich mines in this region. Some sceptics think that the idea of gryphons originates from the fossilized remains of beaked dinosaurs that are sometimes found in this area.

HERALDIC EMBLEMS

Pliny the Elder included the gryphon in his *Natural History* during the 1st century AD. This ensured its later popularity among medieval Europeans, for whom it became an embodiment of noble ferocity and courage, combining intelligence with strength.

SIZE COMPARISON

LENGTH: 3m (10ft)
WINGSPAN: 4m (13ft)
WEIGHT: 180kg (400lb)

999790790.789.7

6360387-080-0-327A49   70790-789.7---8789468968940.0.0

THE MONGOLIAN DEATH WORM

Hidden in the shifting sands of the Gobi Desert lies an unseen but much feared beast – the *allghoi khorkhoi* or 'death worm'. This enormous red worm, growing up to 1.5 metres (5ft) long, has formidable twin weapons – deadly acidic saliva that it spits at its prey, and an ability to kill or at least stun at greater distances through a high-voltage electrical discharge.

EVIDENCE

ON THE TRAIL OF THE DEATH WORM
News of the death worm first reached the west through the accounts of Roy Chapman Andrews, a palaeontologist who searched for fossil deposits in the Gobi desert during the 1920s. Chapman's adventures later inspired the fictional heroics of Indiana Jones.

POSSIBLE IDENTITIES?
There are various theories to explain this bizarre creature, but it is almost certainly not a true worm, since it would swiftly dry out in the harsh desert conditions. Possibilities include a limbless lizard, a venomous snake, or even an electric eel that has adapted to land.

999790790.789.7

DISTRIBUTION

The death worm is restricted to the southern Gobi Desert, from Mongolia into northern China.

HABITAT The worm is most common in hot valleys with deep-rooted saxaul trees. Perhaps it makes use of the plant's ability to store water for long periods.

DIET Death worms probably use their venom and electric shocks to subdue small desert mammals before eating them.

TRACKS AND SIGNS

The death worm spends most of its time below ground, and its burrows are swiftly hidden by the shifting sands. It is most commonly seen above ground during the rainy season, perhaps forced to the surface as the soil becomes waterlogged.

POTENTIAL RISK: EXTREME

While tales of the death worm's attacks are probably exaggerated, the creature is apparently such a swift killer that it is best avoided.

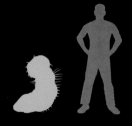

SIZE COMPARISON

HEIGHT: 90cm (3t)
LENGTH: 1.5m (5ft)
WEIGHT: 30kg (66lb)

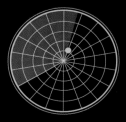

PROXIMITY STATUS

WARNING: SUBJECT HIGHLY AGGRESSIVE – CHECK SAFETY CLOTHING AND RETREAT SLOWLY

BAD LUCK?
Mongolian natives of the Gobi Desert consider the *allghoi khorkhoi* so terrible that even to hear its name is considered bad luck.

HISTORIC RECORD

1900AD

1926 Roy Chapman Andrews describes the worm in his book *On the Trail of Ancient Man.*

1920AD

1940AD

1960AD

1990 Czech explorer Ivan Mackerle mounts the first of two expeditions in search of the death worm.

1980AD

2003–4 Two more western expeditions collect local tales of the death worm, but fail to find the creature itself.

2000AD

PRESENT DAY

Naga traditions are spread across south Asia, perhaps suggesting a wider distribution of these huge serpents in earlier times.

THE NAGA

Serpent gods called *naga* are worshipped by Buddhists and Hindus alike across much of south Asia. The people of Thailand and Laos have a stronger belief than most, backed up by their insistence that the *naga* is a living creature. This enormous crested serpent is said to spend much of its life in underground caverns, but occasionally emerges to frighten humans and livestock near the Mekong River.

TRACKS AND SIGNS

Coming and going mostly by water, the *naga* leaves no tracks in its wake. However, Thai traditions link it to the so-called '*naga* lights', glowing fireballs that emerge from the Mekong River every October.

300 —

250 —

200 —

150 —

➤

100 —

POTENTIAL RISK: HIGH

The variety of local traditions associated with the *naga*, both positive and negative, suggests that despite its size, this serpent does not present a threat to humans except when angered. However, Buddhist accounts of the *naga* say that they are capable of killing both through the injection of poison and with their constricting coils.

50 —

0 —

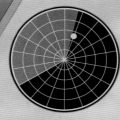

PROXIMITY STATUS

SUBJECT STATIC BUT AGGRESSIVE – DO NOT PROVOKE

HABITAT *Naga* sightings are usually in or close to rivers. They are thought to spend much of their time in subterranean caverns linked to the river systems.

DIET Like other large snakes, *naga* probably prey mostly on deer and other forest animals. A serpent of this size can go for weeks or months without a kill.

01001 1101
_10011101
010000

CRESTED SERPENT

Descriptions of the *naga* consistently describe a crest of some sort on the animal's head, which it raises when angered.

999790790.789.7

HISTORIC RECORD

1968 Possible date of an unsourced photo, widely circulated in Thailand, that shows a group of US servicemen holding an enormous, eel-like animal.

1960ᴀᴅ

1992 Workmen rebuilding a temple in the Phon Piasi region allegedly disturb a *naga*.

1980ᴀᴅ

1997 Police chief Suphat and many others see a *naga* in the Mekong River near Phon Piasi.

2000ᴀᴅ

2006 Large crowds gather to watch a supposed *naga* in the river at Nong Khai.

PRESENT DAY

EVIDENCE

NAGA QUEST

In 2000, British researcher Richard Freeman of Britain's Centre for Fortean Zoology travelled to Thailand in search of the *naga*. Although he found no firm evidence, he spoke to many reputable witnesses. They included a local police chief who had seen an enormous snake swimming in the river, and a village elder who recalled a close encounter with a *naga* in a local cave.

POSSIBLE IDENTITIES?

Some people have suggested the *naga* seen in rivers could be a giant oarfish (see p.101). But Freeman proposed that it could be a madtsoid – part of a group of huge primitive snakes that evolved alongside the dinosaurs. They survived in Australia until about 10,000 years ago.

SIZE COMPARISON

HEIGHT: 4m (13ft)
LENGTH: 9m (30ft)
WEIGHT: 350kg (770lb)

6360387-080-0.3278646584940 - - - - - 999790790.789.7 - - - 8789468968940.0.0

300 —

250 —

200 —

AUTO 150 —

➤

100 —

50 —

0 —

YETI

Himalayan villagers have long told tales of an enormous hairy wildman that haunts the upper slopes of the mountains. Occasionally even outsiders have seen its enormous footprints. Today, the yeti is one of the most famous of all the world's fantastic creatures, but it was largely unknown until 1921, when Lieutenant-Colonel Charles Howard-Bury discovered strange footprints in the snow at an altitude of 6500m (21,000ft), and the legend of the 'abominable snowman' was born. In fact, the yeti had been recorded before – several Victorian travellers reported native stories of an ape-like creature living in the snow.

TRACKS AND SIGNS

Yetis usually hide from people, revealing their presence through their tell-tale footprints. On the rare occasions when they are seen, it is usually as a dark, lumbering shape moving across a distant snow field.

EVIDENCE

SCALPS AND HANDS
The monks of Nepal's Pangboche Monastery keep a shrine containing an alleged yeti scalp, though scientists believe it is made of yak skin. Other traces are more promising – hair samples brought back by explorers seem to resemble an unknown primate. And a 'yeti hand' was stolen from Pangboche in the 1990s, shortly after a study had suggested its tissue was not human, but 'near-human'.

FOOTPRINTS IN THE SNOW
Many mountaineers in the Himalayas claim to have seen giant footprints – including Sir Edmund Hillary and Tenzing Norgay during the first ascent of Everest in 1953. Two years earlier, Eric Shipton took a famous photo of a footprint with his ice axe for scale (below). Shipton and his colleagues followed a trail of prints for almost a mile. Sceptical scientists say they are distorted bear tracks, but the shape, and in particular the enormous 'big toe', seem far more ape-like.

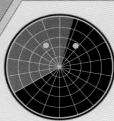

PROXIMITY STATUS

SUBJECT WARY – MAINTAIN DISTANCE AND DO NOT ALARM

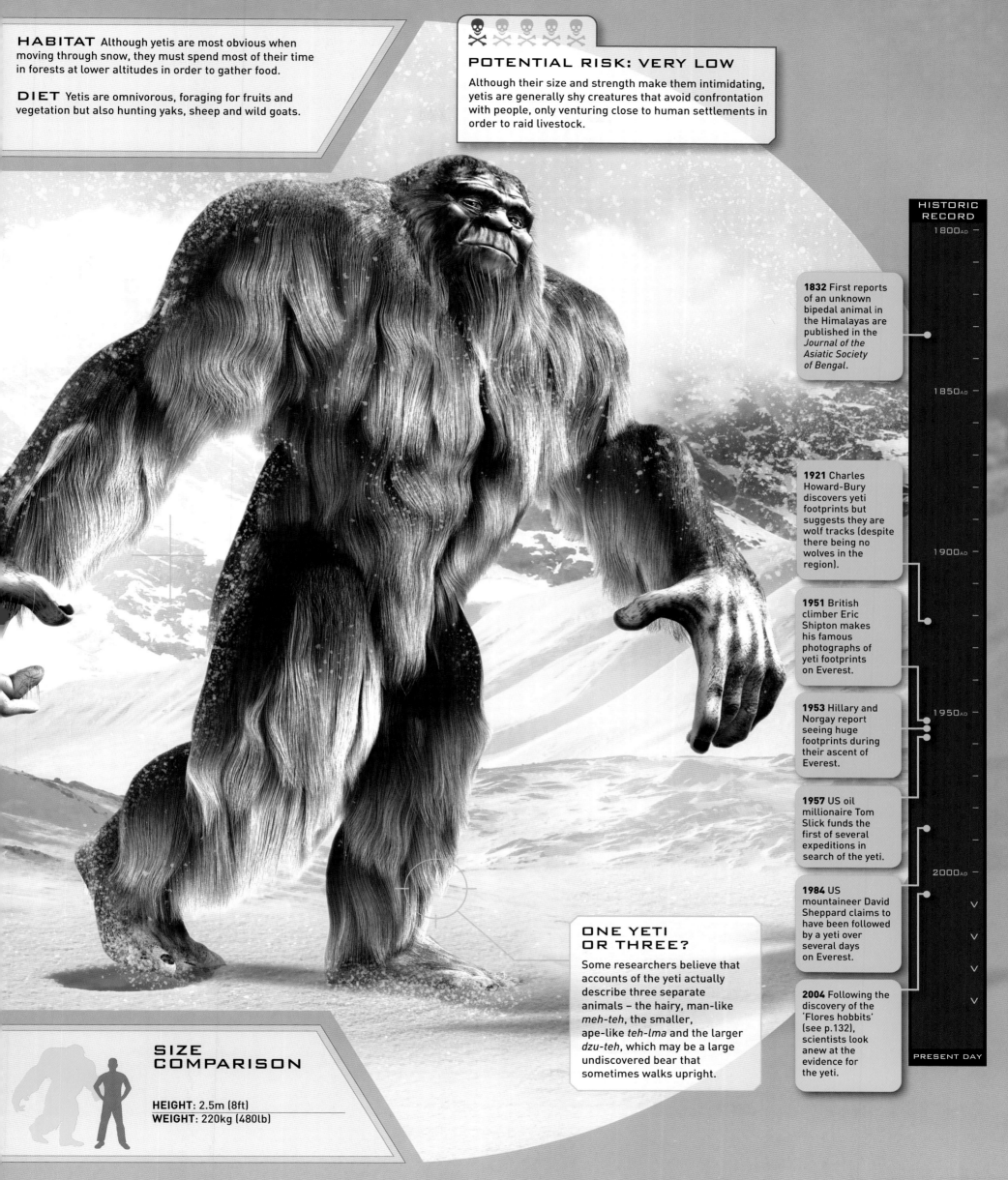

HABITAT Although yetis are most obvious when moving through snow, they must spend most of their time in forests at lower altitudes in order to gather food.

DIET Yetis are omnivorous, foraging for fruits and vegetation but also hunting yaks, sheep and wild goats.

POTENTIAL RISK: VERY LOW

Although their size and strength make them intimidating, yetis are generally shy creatures that avoid confrontation with people, only venturing close to human settlements in order to raid livestock.

ONE YETI OR THREE?

Some researchers believe that accounts of the yeti actually describe three separate animals – the hairy, man-like *meh-teh*, the smaller, ape-like *teh-lma* and the larger *dzu-teh*, which may be a large undiscovered bear that sometimes walks upright.

SIZE COMPARISON

HEIGHT: 2.5m (8ft)
WEIGHT: 220kg (480lb)

HISTORIC RECORD

1800AD

1832 First reports of an unknown bipedal animal in the Himalayas are published in the *Journal of the Asiatic Society of Bengal*.

1850AD

1921 Charles Howard-Bury discovers yeti footprints but suggests they are wolf tracks (despite there being no wolves in the region).

1900AD

1951 British climber Eric Shipton makes his famous photographs of yeti footprints on Everest.

1953 Hillary and Norgay report seeing huge footprints during their ascent of Everest.

1950AD

1957 US oil millionaire Tom Slick funds the first of several expeditions in search of the yeti.

1984 US mountaineer David Sheppard claims to have been followed by a yeti over several days on Everest.

2000AD

2004 Following the discovery of the 'Flores hobbits' (see p.132), scientists look anew at the evidence for the yeti.

PRESENT DAY

129

16390456759850.098.08e83r93.00/43740.9-93776767------2789690749B7.97979

TRAVELLERS' TALES

Before the great explorers opened up the world from the 1400s, most western ideas about the exotic lands of the Indian Ocean and beyond relied on third-hand reports passed on from a few well-travelled merchants and pilgrims. These imaginative accounts filled the mysterious east with some of the most bizarre and fantastical creatures ever recorded– but could some of these freakish beasts have really existed?

In the year 1357 a medieval bestseller was published. *The Travels of Sir John Mandeville* claimed to be a travel journal in the tradition of Marco Polo, recounting the travels of a mercenary knight in Egypt, India, China and beyond. For about 100 years, Mandeville's book was second only to the Bible in popularity, yet by the 1600s he was widely regarded as 'the greatest liar of all time', and today it's thought that the Anglo-French knight who supposedly wrote the work never even existed.

Mandeville's fantasies had been exposed by three centuries of exploration and discovery that revealed a real Asia very different from the place he described. But even if Mandeville's writings were made up, they often summarized ideas about the east that had been around for centuries before.

Probably the most long-lived of Mandeville's strange peoples are the 'dog-heads' – humans with the heads of jackals or dogs. The best known 'dog-head' is probably the god Anubis from ancient Egypt, but in medieval times there were strange traditions that the well-known Christian St Christopher was actually a giant with the head of a dog.

Other strange beings include faun-like wildmen, cyclopes, cannibals, and people whose faces grow below their shoulders. Mandeville also writes about the sciapodes – dwarf-like people who hop around on a single enormous foot which they also use to shield themselves from the Sun, and the Panotti, who use their huge, rabbit-like ears for the same purpose. Some peoples described by Mandeville appear more human,

but have equally bizarre habits. There is a tribe that nourishes itself through the smell of apples alone, and a race of pygmies with mouths so small they have to take all their food through reed straws.

The strange stories of Sir John Mandeville have puzzled historians for centuries. His descriptions of geography are accurate, even if his tales of strange creatures seem unlikely. Some think that Mandeville was actually a French surgeon who spent some time in Egypt, and collected tales of the far east from merchants and missionaries. Many of the monsters he describes seem to originate much further back, with the first-century *Natural History* of the Roman writer Pliny the Elder, but others seem to be Mandeville's own . Are they inventions of his own vivid imagination, or a rare record of another traveller's encounters?

EVIDENCE

IN SEARCH OF THE DOG-HEADS
Cryptozoologist Bernard Heuvelmans had an intriguing idea about the origins of at least one of Mandeville's strange creatures. He suggested that stories of encounters with dog-headed humans were inspired by sightings of the strange animals of Madagascar. This isolated island is the only home to a group of primates known as lemurs (right), which have monkey-like bodies but long and somewhat dog-like faces. Some of them even move across the ground in an upright 'dance' that looks remarkably human. Today only smaller species survive, but there were once much larger lemurs, including the gorilla-sized *Megaladapis*. What would medieval travellers have made of creatures that had the general proportions of a human, but the elongated face of a dog?

SIZE COMPARISON

HEIGHT: 2.1m (7ft)
WEIGHT: 100kg (220lb)

98509.098.08e83r93.00/43740.9-93776767------278969074987.97979.08735 2799

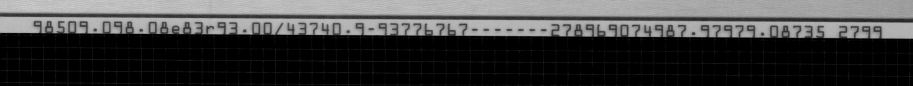

DISTRIBUTION

Reports have tended to place strange humanoid creatures in the Indian Ocean and southeast Asia, but similar rumours are found around the world.

This illustration from a 15th-century *Book of Marvels* shows a race of civilized but dog-headed people, believed at the time to live on the Isle of Agaman in the Gulf of Bengal, off the coast of India.

Early engravings show the huge variety of fantastic creatures said to live in the 'Mysterious East', from crane-necked and beaked humanoids to people with their faces embedded in their chest or no heads at all!

HISTORIC RECORD

c.1010 German bishop Walther von Speyer writes an account of the life of St Christopher that portrays the saint as a dog-headed giant.

1000ᴀᴅ

1100ᴀᴅ

1247 Franciscan friar Joannes de Plano returns from a mission to the east, and writes of the Mongol chief Ogedei Khan's battles with a tribe of dog-headed men.

1200ᴀᴅ

c.1300 A *Mappa Mundi* (map of the world) completed for Hereford Cathedral depicts many of the monsters later described by Mandeville.

1300ᴀᴅ

1357 The *Travels of Sir John Mandeville* is published, and becomes an instant bestseller.

1400ᴀᴅ

1500ᴀᴅ

v
v
v
v

PRESENT DAY

The *orang pendek* is confined to the island of Sumatra, but older tales of small hairy men are found on other nearby islands.

ORANG PENDEK

For centuries, the forest-dwelling Suku Anak Dalam people of central Sumatra, Indonesia, have shared their lives with a small hairy creature they know as the *orang pendek* or 'short person'. Descriptions of this animal are always the same – including the intriguing fact that it walks upright on two legs. It has also been seen by nearby villagers and western explorers. Many scientists now believe that Sumatra really is home to an undiscovered ape, and discoveries from a nearby island have inspired serious efforts to identify and protect the *orang pendek* before it is too late.

300 –

250 –

200 –

AUTO 150 –

➤

100 –

50 –

0 –

PRIMATE OR HOMINID?

Various features suggest that *orang pendek* is an ape, like the chimp and gibbon. The idea that it might be a hominid – a direct relative of humans – is more controversial. Until this elusive creature is caught on film, or a body is found, we simply can't know for certain how it fits into our family tree.

EVIDENCE

PRINTS AND FUR
Expeditions to Sumatra in 2001 and 2003 recovered footprint casts and hair samples that could not be matched with any known species. They appear to be from an unknown ape.

LIVING HOBBITS?
In 2003, archaeologists working on the nearby island of Flores announced the discovery of a species of small humans that flourished until just a few thousand years ago. They were soon nicknamed 'hobbits' but are now known as *Homo floresiensis*. Is it possible that these people survive today as the *orang pendek*?

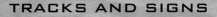

TRACKS AND SIGNS

The *orang pendek*'s footprints have been described as a unique mix of gibbon, orang utan, chimp and human. Their fur is usually described as reddish, although there are some variations.

PROXIMITY STATUS

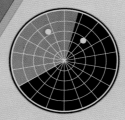

SUBJECTS ALARMED BUT NOT AGGRESSIVE – AVOID SUDDEN MOVEMENT

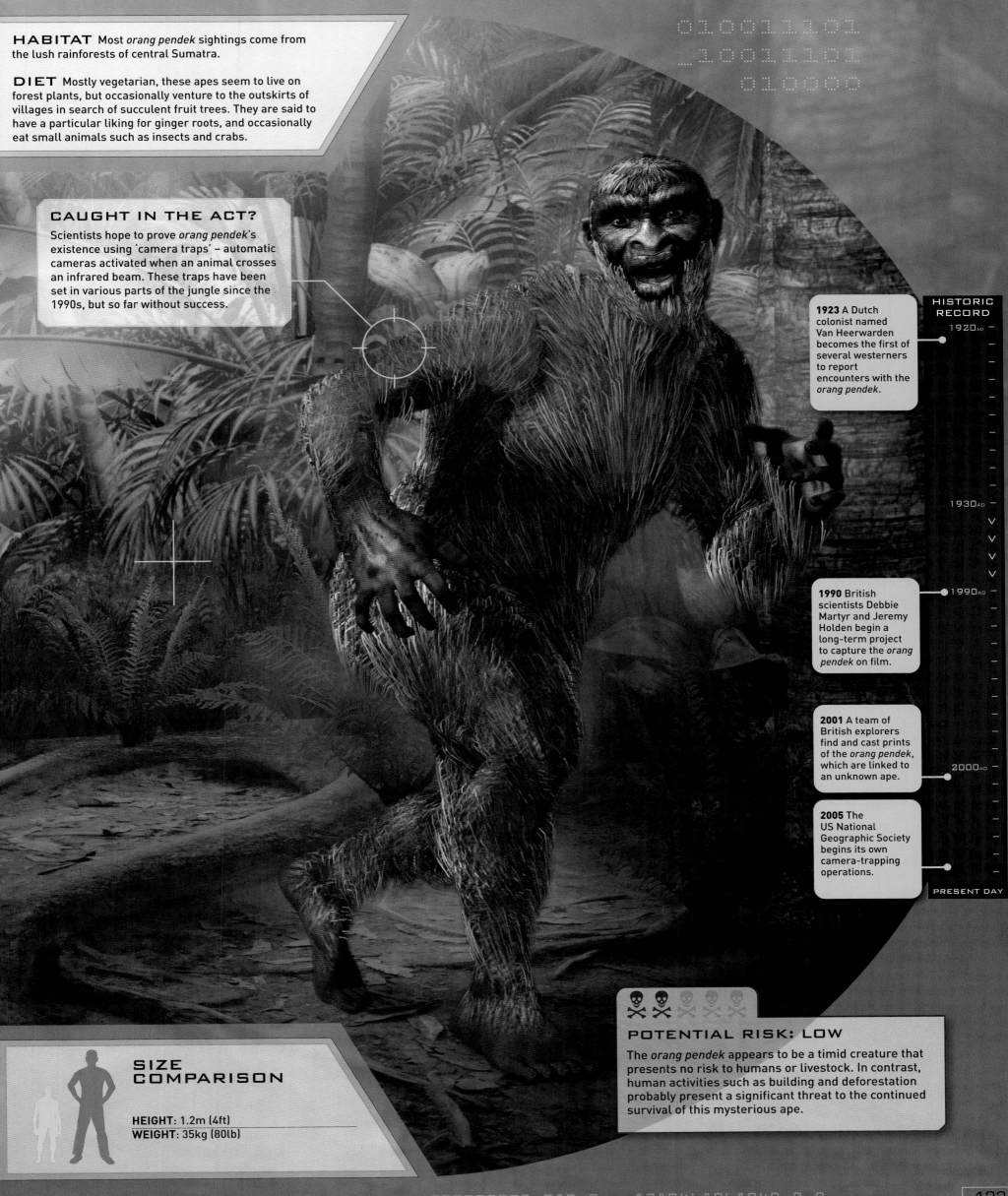

HABITAT Most *orang pendek* sightings come from the lush rainforests of central Sumatra.

DIET Mostly vegetarian, these apes seem to live on forest plants, but occasionally venture to the outskirts of villages in search of succulent fruit trees. They are said to have a particular liking for ginger roots, and occasionally eat small animals such as insects and crabs.

CAUGHT IN THE ACT?

Scientists hope to prove *orang pendek*'s existence using 'camera traps' – automatic cameras activated when an animal crosses an infrared beam. These traps have been set in various parts of the jungle since the 1990s, but so far without success.

HISTORIC RECORD

1920AD

1923 A Dutch colonist named Van Heerwarden becomes the first of several westerners to report encounters with the *orang pendek*.

1930AD

1990 British scientists Debbie Martyr and Jeremy Holden begin a long-term project to capture the *orang pendek* on film.

1990AD

2001 A team of British explorers find and cast prints of the *orang pendek*, which are linked to an unknown ape.

2000AD

2005 The US National Geographic Society begins its own camera-trapping operations.

PRESENT DAY

POTENTIAL RISK: LOW

The *orang pendek* appears to be a timid creature that presents no risk to humans or livestock. In contrast, human activities such as building and deforestation probably present a significant threat to the continued survival of this mysterious ape.

SIZE COMPARISON

HEIGHT: 1.2m (4ft)
WEIGHT: 35kg (80lb)

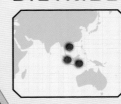

Although the *orang bati* is local to the island of Ceram, there are reports of similar bat-like entities from as far away as Vietnam.

ORANG BATI

The people of the Indonesian island of Ceram live in fear of a humanoid creature with bat-like wings, which emerges from its lair on Mount Kairatu at night and swoops down on unsuspecting villages to abduct small children. They call this creature *orang bati* ('the winged man'), but most accounts describe it as being more like a fur-covered monkey than a man. Similar giant bat-like beings are described from other southeast Asian countries, but it seems that only on Ceram have they become fearsome predators.

300 —

250 —

200 —

AUTO   150 —

➤

100 —

50 —

0 —

MAN BAT

Descriptions of the *orang bati* suggest its body is roughly 1.5m (5ft) long with an enormous span of bat-like wings covered in black fur.

POTENTIAL RISK: HIGH

If the stories of child abductions are taken at face value, then the *orang bati* must be a fearsome and dangerous predator. However, it's also possible that a relatively harmless giant bat has become associated with other local scare stories.

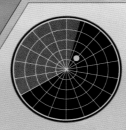

PROXIMITY STATUS

WARNING: SUBJECT IN FLIGHT AT HIGH SPEED – EVASIVE ACTION REQUIRED

HABITAT The *orang bati* is thought to nest in the extinct volcano of Mount Kairatu.

DIET The creature's apparent habit of abducting small children on Ceram may be explained by the island's lack of other small primates – elsewhere similar creatures may prey on monkeys.

HISTORIC RECORD

1900AD

1925 Explorer Ernest Bartels sees a giant bat known as the *ahool*, reported by natives to eat fish, in Java's Salek Mountains.

1920AD

1940AD

1960AD

TRACKS AND SIGNS

A night-time hunter that swoops without warning on coastal villages such as Uraur, the *orang bati* leaves no trace behind. It is only occasionally seen but its call, a mournful wail, can sometimes be heard in the foothills of Mount Kairatu.

1987 Tyson Hughes collects local tales of the *orang bati*, and searches for its lair without success.

1980AD

2000AD

PRESENT DAY

EVIDENCE

MISSIONARY SIGHTINGS
Most of the accounts of the *orang bati* that have reached the outside world come from missionaries and later voluntary workers who have ventured to these remote islands. One such volunteer, Englishman Tyson Hughes, collected local tales of the giant bat creature in the 1980s and came to believe in its reality after seeing it himself.

POSSIBLE IDENTITIES?
Although the villagers of Ceram insist that the *orang bati* is a flying humanoid, there are no flying primates known to science. Other possibilities include a giant form of fruitbat (right), or even a surviving pterosaur like *Kongamato* (see p.116). Indeed, there is now good evidence that some large pterosaurs had developed their own form of 'fur'.

SIZE COMPARISON

HEIGHT: 1.5m (5ft)
WINGSPAN: 4m (13ft)
WEIGHT: 50kg (110lb)

456754854504.048.08e83r43.00/43740.4-43776767-------278464807
3.00/43740.9-93776767------278969074987.97979.08735

ISSIE

Japan has countless strange creatures in its folklore, but the most famous animal with a claim to reality is the monster of Lake Ikeda, a deep, water-filled volcanic crater on the southern island of Kyushu. Named 'Issie' in imitation of Scotland's 'Nessie', this 10-metre-long animal has the classic characteristics of a lake monster – a small horse-like head, flippers and a long, humped body. Legends of a creature in the lake go back for centuries, but recent sightings began in the 1970s. Despite numerous attempts to capture Issie on video or film, she remains elusive.

EVIDENCE

LEGENDARY ORIGIN
Japanese folklore contains many tales of sea monsters, such as the giant carp of Lake Biwa (right). Issie was supposedly a beautiful white mare who roamed the shores of Lake Ikeda, until one day a samurai warrior stole her beloved foal. In despair, she threw herself into the lake, where grief transformed her into an enormous monster.

FAMILY SIGHTING
One of the most impressive sightings of Issie came in 1978, when more than 20 members of one extended family, enjoying a lakeside picnic, observed two large black humps moving through the water for some four minutes.

999790790.789.7

DISTRIBUTION

Issie is confined to a single lake on Japan's Kyushu Island. Intriguingly the lake has no connections to other rivers, so how the creature got there is a mystery.

HABITAT The creature is said to live just below the lake's surface, frequently coming up for air or to inspect its surroundings.

DIET Given the size of Lake Ikeda, Issie can presumably sustain herself by feeding on fish.

TRACKS AND SIGNS
Although reports of Issie at the lake's surface are quite frequent, they usually consist of one or more large humps – sightings of the creature's head are rare.

☠ ☠ ☠ ☠ ☠

POTENTIAL RISK: VERY LOW
Whatever she is, Issie appears to have no interest in humans and there are no reports of aggressive behaviour.

SIZE COMPARISON

LENGTH: 12m (40ft)
WEIGHT: 4000kg (9,000lb)

PROXIMITY STATUS

SUBJECT SURFACING – MAINTAIN POSITION AND PREPARE FOR WATER TURBULENCE

1639045675985009.098.08e83r43.00/43740.9-93776767------278969074987.97979.08735

EEL OR WATER HORSE?

Issie's supposed origins place her firmly in a group of Japanese sea and lake monsters known as 'water horses'. However, Lake Ikeda is also home to eels that grow to more than 2m (6ft) long, and some have suggested that Issie herself is in fact an even larger 'monster eel'.

1978 Members of the Yutaka family observe Issie, triggering a wave of interest in Lake Ikeda's legendary monster.

1991 A video alleged to show Issie emerges, but with no indication of scale it may simply show one of the lake's outsized eels.

1990s–2000s Sightings of Issie continue and creatures are still filmed in the lake, but no conclusive evidence emerges.

ROGUE CROC?

Sceptical researchers have suggested that sightings of giant reptiles may in fact be saltwater crocodiles, which can grow to more than 6m (20ft) long. However, *Megalania* reports often come from well outside the crocodile's known range, and the different postures of crocodiles and lizards should make cases of mistaken identity unlikely.

COW KILLER?

In 1968, soldiers training in the Queensland rainforest came across the body of a cow in a remote swampy region. The animal had literally been torn in half by some huge predator, and enormous lizard tracks were found nearby.

16390456759850**9**.098.08e83r93.00/43740.9-93776767------27896907
e83r93.00/43740.9-93776767------278969074987.97979.08735

MEGALANIA

An enormous reptilian predator, some seven metres (23ft) long and weighing as much as a tonne, sounds like something from the age of the dinosaurs. But the shocking truth is that this monster roamed Australia until just 40,000 years ago, surviving long enough to be a threat to early aboriginal settlers on the continent. *Megalania prisca* was an enormous monitor lizard or 'goanna', far larger than even the surviving Komodo dragon from the islands of Indonesia. And many people believe that this giant never became truly extinct. Countless reports of huge reptiles across Australia suggest that *Megalania* might still be out there.

HISTORIC
RECORD
1960ᴀᴅ —

October 1968
Soldiers encounter a supposed *Megalania* 'kill' during training in Queensland.

1970ᴀᴅ —

1979 Herpetologist Frank Gordon sees a giant lizard in the Watagan mountains of New South Wales.

1980ᴀᴅ —

1986 Campers at the Ashburton River in Victoria discover and measure the prints of an enormous lizard.

1990ᴀᴅ —

PRESENT DAY

EVIDENCE

EXPERT WITNESS
One of the most convincing reports of an Australian giant reptile came in 1979, when herpetologist (reptile scientist) Frank Gordon startled a huge lizard with the sound of his car engine. Gordon estimated the length of the creature, which he had earlier assumed was a large fallen log, at 8–9m (27–30ft).

THE ELUSIVE BUNYIP
Aboriginal traditions include many tales of the bunyip, a strange monster that usually lives in lakes (right). Some have suggested that, if the surviving giant lizards are partly amphibious, it might explain some of these stories.

999790790.789.7

TRACKS AND SIGNS

While they cannot be conclusively linked to sightings of *Megalania*, various reports of oversized lizard prints with a tail dragged between them may well be tracks left by Australia's mysterious giant reptiles.

DISTRIBUTION

Reports of surviving giant lizards are concentrated in Queensland, New South Wales and Victoria. Giant goannas are also found on New Guinea.

HABITAT *Megalania* seems to inhabit poorly explored rainforest areas and the surrounding bush.

DIET These enormous reptiles evolved to hunt giant kangaroos that went extinct during the last ice age. Today they must survive on smaller prey of various kinds, though they occasionally attack domestic livestock such as cattle.

SIZE COMPARISON

HEIGHT: 1.8m (6ft)
LENGTH: 7m (23ft)
WEIGHT: 1000kg (2200lb)

PROXIMITY STATUS

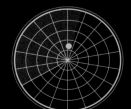

SUBJECT ALARMED, AGGRESSIVE AND FAST-MOVING – WITHDRAW!

POTENTIAL RISK: HIGH

Although they spend much of their time resting, monitor lizards are capable of sudden bursts of speed and action that make them dangerous predators. Several monitor species, including the Komodo dragon, are also known to inject potent venom when they bite.

DISTRIBUTION

Yowies have been reported from across Australia, and seem to be especially common in eastern regions.

THE YOWIE

Ever since the first convicts arrived in Australia in the late 18th century, there have been occasional sighting of a strange, almost comical creature that seems similar to the North American Bigfoot. Known affectionately as the Yowie, this solitary animal has an enormous body, tiny head, spindly legs and huge feet. While aboriginal tales depict the Yowie as a fearsome and vicious wildman, most western encounters suggest that it behaves like other large apes, and favours intimidating displays over outright aggression.

EVIDENCE

ENCOUNTER BY FIRELIGHT

In 1912 travelling surveyor Charles Harper gave the *Sydney Sun* newspaper a report of a lengthy encounter with a strange ape-like creature that came to the edge of his camp in the Currickbilly Mountains of New South Wales. He recalled an animal as tall as a man but bulkier, covered in reddish-brown hair and with a pendulous stomach hanging down almost to its knees. This bizarre creature attempted to frighten away Harper and his companions with a series of chilling screams and a threatening display of chest beating, but eventually retreated without a direct attack.

TRACKS AND SIGNS

The Yowie's elusive nature means that direct sightings are rare, but the animal can often be tracked using its enormous footprints or the pungent smell it leaves hanging in the air.

POTENTIAL RISK: MEDIUM

Although most Yowie encounters are peaceful, the animal is enormously powerful and capable of acting violently when provoked. Attacks on dogs and livestock have been reported, and humans should approach with caution.

PROXIMITY STATUS

SUBJECT PASSIVE – APPROACH BUT DO NOT DISTURB

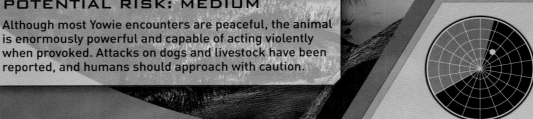

HABITAT These ape-like creatures tend to live in remote mountainous and forested areas.

DIET Yowies are thought to be largely vegetarian but are probably omnivorous, eating whatever they come across. Some recent reports have linked them to attacks on livestock.

A MARSUPIAL APE?

The Yowie's ape-like appearance suggests that, like Bigfoot and the yeti, it could be a close 'hominid' relative of our own species. But some experts believe that this strange beast could be an example of 'convergent evolution' – a marsupial mammal that has evolved independently over millions of years of isolation to resemble a hominid.

HISTORIC RECORD

1800AD

1835 First report of a wildman called the 'Yahoo' feared by the Aborigines.

1850AD

1871 George Osborne becomes the first white man to see a Yowie near Avondale, New South Wales.

1900AD

1912 Charles Harper encounters a Yowie in the mountains of New South Wales.

1950AD

1977 20 school pupils see a Yowie while camping at Springbrook, Queensland.

1993 A wave of Yowie sightings begins around the Blue Mountains of New South Wales.

2000AD

PRESENT DAY

AUSTRALIAN BIGFOOT

Many eyewitnesses to Yowie encounters have emphasized the animal's unusual, outsized feet. Casts of footprints also seem to suggest it has an opposable big toe, arranged in the same way as a human thumb, which it may use for grasping food.

SIZE COMPARISON

HEIGHT: 2.2m (7ft)
WEIGHT: 140kg (310lb)

GLOSSARY

Amphisbaenid
Also known as 'worm lizards', amphisbaenids are a type of reptile that has evolved to lose its limbs. They look rather like snakes,but the disappearance of their limbs seems to have happened independently, most likely to help these loose-skinned burrowing creatures move more easily through the earth.

Ape
An animal in the primate family that is a close relative of humans. Apes include gibbons, orang utans, chimpanzees, gorillas, and humans themselves.

Arabian Nights
A rich collection of Persian, Middle Eastern and Indian folktales, first translated into a European language by Frenchman Antoine Galland during the early 1700s.

Australasia
A collective term for the large southern continent that contains the major islands of Australia, New Zealand and New Guinea, along with smaller outlying islands.

Biped
Any animal that moves around for most of the time on two legs rather than four. Humans, kangaroos and some dinosaurs are or were bipedal, and other apes are bipedal some of the time.

Cartilage
A tough, hardened body tissue found in most animals, but which makes up the entire skeleton of sharks, rays and similar fish.

Constrictor
A type of snake that kills its prey by wrapping around an animal and tightening or constricting its coils so that the victim can no longer breathe. The largest snakes, such as boas and anacondas, tend to use constriction rather than venom to kill their prey.

Cryptozoologist
A researcher who attempts to discover the reality behind stories of undiscovered animals and fantastical creatures, through historical study, interviews with eyewitnesses and exploration.

Dinosaur
A special group of reptiles that were the dominant life on dry land for 160 million years. Dinosaurs are distinguished by features of their skeletons and hip joints, and have officially been extinct for 65 million years.

Ecosystem
An interconnected web of living species that rely on each other for their existence within a particular habitat. This might include plants, plant-eating animals, predators, scavengers and parasites.

Electromagnetism
A force that can create both electrical and magnetic effects. Strong electromagnetic fields can cause delicate electronics to go haywire, and some think that they can also effect the human brain, causing a range of illusions and strange feelings.

Eurasia
A collective term for the continents of Europe and Asia together, recognizing the fact that they merge into one another along the line of the Ural Mountains in western Russia.

Fort, Charles (1874-1932)
A pioneering US researcher into anomalies – discoveries and phenomena that do not fit in with the picture of the world established by science and common sense. Fort's interests ranged from ghosts to rains of frogs, and from unknown animals to lights in the sky. The word 'Fortean' is often used to define a sceptical yet open-minded approach to such phenomena.

Fossil
The remains of an animal or plant that have been preserved first by burial in sand or mud that compresses to form rock, and then by replacement of the original 'organic' material with durable rocky minerals that take the same shape.

Genus
A group containing several closely related species. Modern humans are a species (*Homo sapiens*) within the genus *Homo*.

Heuvelmans, Bernard (1916-2001)
A Belgian-French zoologist and explorer who spend much of his life investigating the evidence for undiscovered animals, and who coined the term 'cryptozoology' to describe this field of research. His 1955 book *On the Track of Unknown Animals* is still one of the best works on the subject.

Habitat
The natural environment in which a creature prefers to live, and where it finds food, shelter and a mate.

Hominid
A modern human being (in the species *Homo sapiens*) or any close relative. The scientific definition of hominids includes gorillas, chimpanzees and orang utans, but the term is more often used to describe extinct species that are more closely related to humans – ape-men called australopithecines, and extinct members of the genus *Homo* such as Neanderthal man (*Homo neanderthalensis*) and the Flores 'hobbits' (*Homo floresiensis*).

Hybrid
Any creature that contains a mix of features from two or more different animals. The Chimera, Minotaur and cockatrice are all hybrids.

Mammal
An animal distinguished by features such as furry skin, a means of keeping its body temperature even, and the ability to produce milk for its young.

Marsupial
A mammal that gives birth to underdeveloped young that are then raised in a protective pouch on the mother's belly. Today marsupials are found in Australasia and South America, but they were once far more widespread.

Mesopotamia
A region of fertile land in modern-day Iraq, between the Tigris and Euphrates rivers, which gave rise to many of the earliest civilizations.

One Thousand and One Nights
The original Persian title of the *Arabian Nights*.

Palaeontologist
An expert in the excavation and study of fossils and prehistoric life.

Plesiosaur
A marine reptile from the time of the dinosaurs, distinguished by a bulky body with flippers, and a long neck with a small head. Plesiosaurs have officially been extinct for 65 million years or more, but they are the closest known matches to many descriptions of sea serpents and lake monsters.

Primate
A group of mammals distinguished by features including relatively large brains and stereoscopic vision (thanks to a pair of forward-facing eyes). The primates include lemurs, monkeys, apes and humans.

Pterosaur
A flying reptile from the time of the dinosaurs, with bat-like wing membranes stretched across modified finger bones. Pterosaurs have officially been extinct for 65 million years, but reports of flying reptile-like creatures persist.

Reptile
An animal distinguished by features such as smooth or scaly skin without fur, and the fact that it lays eggs rather than giving birth to live young.

Sauropod
A group of large, four-legged, plant-eating dinosaurs with elephant-like bodies, long necks with small heads, and long tails. Sauropods match the description of various giant reptiles supposedly living in the jungles of Africa, but they have been officially extinct for 65 million years.

Salamander
A group of amphibians (animals that split their lives between land and water), with slim bodies, moist skins and long tails. Folklore often associates salamanders with fire, but in recent times these animals have been suggested as a possible identity for the European *tatzelwurm*.

Scandinavia
A region of northern Europe consisting of the countries of Denmark, Norway and Sweden. Scandinavia was homeland to the Vikings, and colonists carried Scandinavian culture to Iceland.

Species
A group of living organisms that are able to interbreed with each other and produce 'viable' offspring (ones that are healthy and can also reproduce). The species is the basic unit of classification among animals, plants and other forms of life. Species are usually given a two-part name, with the first part indicating the wider grouping or genus to which they belong - our own species is called *Homo sapiens* (from the Latin for 'wise man').

Teratorn
A group of enormous birds of prey, with wingspans of up to 8m (26ft), which lived in the Americas up until a few thousand years ago. Closely related to modern condors, surviving teratorns are a favourite explanation for sightings of the giant thunderbird.

UFO
Short for Unidentified Flying Object – any light or moving object in the sky that cannot be identified. Although UFOs are often called 'flying saucers' and some people think they are alien spacecraft visiting Earth, there are other possible explanations, including undiscovered atmospheric animals, and 'Earth lights' associated with natural but undiscovered properties of the Earth itself.

Venom
Any poisonous chemical produced by special glands within an animal and then injected into other animals through a sting or bite. Venom can be used by predators as a weapon of attack, or by otherwise peaceful animals for self defence.

INDEX

163904567598509.098.08e83r93.00/43740.9-93776767------27896907

ACKNOWLEDGEMENTS

Quercus Publishing Plc
21 Bloomsbury Square
London
WC1A 2NS

First published in 2009

A catalogue record of this book is available from the British Library

ISBN 978 1 84866 026 7

Printed and bound in China

10 9 8 7 6 5 4 3 2 1

Text by Giles Sparrow
Illustrations by Pikaia Imaging: www.pikaia-imaging.co.uk
Design and editorial Pikaia Imaging
Proofreading by Hazel Muir

Additional picture credits:

12 The Granger Collection/TopFoto; **32** Shutterstock/Lanbo; **35** Shutterstock/Tim Arbaev;
37 Shutterstock/Randall Stewart; **41** (top) Shutterstock/Keo, (bottom) Corbis; **44** Shutterstock/Janet Quantrill; **46** Shutterstock/Hugo de Wolf; **47** Charles Walker/Topham/TopFoto; **52** Shutterstock/Rostislavv; **53** (bottom) Shutterstock/C., (top) Topham Picturepoint/TopFoto; **54** Mary Evans Picture Library; **58** Fortean/TopFoto; **62** The Granger Collection/TopFoto; **64** Mary Evans Picture Library; **71** Mary Evans Picture Library; **72** Roger-Viollet/TopFoto; **73** Mary Evans Picture Library; **74** Fortean/TopFoto; **76** Fortean/TopFoto; **80** Fortean/TopFoto; **82** Fortean/TopFoto; **84** (left) Fortean/TopFoto; **85** (main image) Fortean/TopFoto, (top) Fortean/TopFoto; **86** Fortean/TopFoto; **88** Fortean/TopFoto; **89** (top) Fortean/TopFoto; **91** (right) Fortean/TopFoto; **92** Fortean/TopFoto; **94** (top) Mary Evans Picture Library, (bottom) University of Florida; **95** Fortean/TopFoto; **96** Fortean/TopFoto; **100** Mary Evans Picture Library; **105** Shutterstock/BW Folsom; **106** Kevin Fleming/Corbis; **107** (top) Mary Evans Picture Library, (bottom) ullsteinbild/TopFoto; **113** Fortean/TopFoto; **115** ImageWorks/TopFoto; **116** Fortean/TopFoto; **119** Photri/TopFoto; **124** The Granger Collection/TopFoto; **127** Shutterstock/William Casey; **128** National Pictures/TopFoto; **130** Shutterstock/Simone van den Berg; **131** (top) World History Archive/TopFoto; **132** Fortean/TopFoto; **135** Shutterstock/Craig Dingle; **136** Mary Evans Picture Library; **139** Fortean/TopFoto; **140** Fortean/TopFoto

163904567598509.098.08e83r93.00/43740.9-93776767------278969074987.97979.08735

DATE DUE

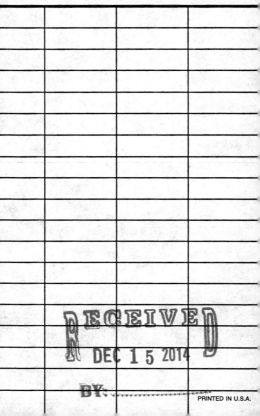

PRINTED IN U.S.A.